DAKOTA GOLD

A story of action and adventure in the West by a great new Western writer!

In a town called Deadwood, anything can happen but nothing much ever does. Until two army deserters are robbed, and revenge sets the town reeling!

Also by Tim Champlin
Published by Ballantine Books:

SUMMER OF THE SIOUX

DAKOTA GOLD

Tim Champlin

BALLANTINE BOOKS • NEW YORK

Library of Congress Catalog Card Number: 82-6666

ISBN 0-345-30529-9

Manufactured in the United States of America

First Ballantine Books Edition: August 1982

For Chris, Kenneth and Liz

CHAPTER 1

It was fear of the Sioux as much as fear of pursuit by the cavalry that caused us to keep our stolen Indian ponies moving as fast as possible. In the blackness, the four of us had to trust our animals' instincts to pick out the way in the unfamiliar terrain. Fortunately, it was mostly undulating prairie, but it was cut up by occasional shallow gullies. In our haste to get away, none of us had thought to bring a compass, and the misty overcast prevented our guiding by the moon or stars.

The loping pony beside me suddenly stumbled in the dark and almost went down. I heard Cathy Jenkins give a startled cry as she was thrown forward and grabbed the pony's neck with both arms.

"Curt! Wiley!" I yelled at the murky forms ahead of me. "Hold up a minute."

I could hear, rather than see, the other two reining up.

"Cathy, are you okay?" Curt Wilder's voice was concerned as he brought his pony up close. The unshod ponies were blowing and snorting, tossing their heads against the restraint of the makeshift hackamores.

"I . . . I'm all right. Just a little tired. My horse nearly fell," she answered, her voice sounding forced and shaky.

"Let's stop and rest here," Curt decided.

"I don't want to hold up the rest of you," she said, a little breathless. "Why don't you all go on. I'll catch up."

"No. We'll stick together. The ponies need rest, anyway," Curt stated, his voice as calm and authoritative, as if he were still commanding his cavalry company. If I hadn't been one of those who'd helped him escape confinement only a couple of hours before, I never would

1

have guessed he had just deserted the Third Cavalry to avoid a court-martial for defying a direct order. "They may not even be chasing us," Curt continued.

"I wouldn't bet on it!" The voice of Cathy's brother, Wiley Jenkins, came out of the darkness. "We almost left our hair in the Big Horns the last time we got cocky."

"How could I forget?" Curt said. "But I don't think the army will be pursuing tonight. Those soldiers are starving, their horses are broken down, and we took them by surprise when we stole these captured ponies. If I know General Buck, he won't let anyone out of that camp tonight, with the Sioux all around—not even for one deserted officer, one mule packer, his sister, and one reporter." I could almost see him grin at me in the dark.

As he spoke, he was helping Cathy to the ground. I groaned when I slid stiffly off the bare back of my Indian pony, still feeling the imprint of his backbone in my backside. "We got anything to hobble these ponies?" I asked. "Sure don't want to be set afoot tonight."

Wiley detached the reins from the bridles and started hobbling their forefeet as the animals dropped their heads to crop the thick prairie grass. "The way we been runnin' 'em, they're pretty winded. I don't think they'd wander far, but we can't take a chance."

By the time Wiley and I had secured the ponies, Cathy and Curt were stretched out on the grass. We flopped down beside them, fatigue beginning to drag at us. We had no food—not even coffee—and no wood for a fire even if we did.

"How far have we come from Slim Buttes?" Cathy asked.

Nobody answered for a moment. Then Curt dug in his pocket for a match to check his watch. He cupped the match to shield the light, even though we appeared to be down in a little swale in the prairie. The brief flare showed the lines that had appeared in Curt's face during the few weeks of the hard summer campaign. He suddenly looked older than his thirty-three years.

Then the match went out and he snapped the watch shut. "At the rate we've been traveling, I'd guess we're about twenty-five miles from camp. The question is, does anybody know how far the Black Hills are?"

"When I interviewed General Buck before we turned south, he told me we were about seven days' march from the Hills. Based on that, I'd say we've got . . . um . . . probably a good sixty miles to go—almost due south," I offered.

Curt grunted. "I just hope we're still headed south. Even Grouard, as good a scout as he is, would have trouble holding some kind of direction in this murk."

"Wish he were here right now," Wiley Jenkins added wistfully. "I believe he could track a bullet in a blizzard."

"You think we're clear of Crazy Horse's band, Curt?" I asked after a little pause.

"Not by a damn sight," Curt snapped. "This country's crawling with Sioux. After they hit us at Slim Buttes a few hours back, they just retired for the night. They haven't gone far. They'll be back to harass the troops with a running battle all the way to the Hills. I just hope we don't blunder into one of their camps out here. They're *mad* clear through."

"This foggy, misty weather will help us if we can slip through 'em," I said.

"We won't make the Hills by daylight, that's sure," Curt replied. "But we need to put as much distance as we can behind us before dawn. It's already one-twenty."

My clothes were still damp and heavy. But they had been wet for so many days, I hardly noticed anymore. As I stretched out on the grass beside Cathy and Curt and closed my eyes, I could feel myself sliding toward an exhausted sleep almost immediately. The murmured conversations began to fade in my ears.

"Let's go, Matt." I was startled awake by a gentle boot toe in the ribs. As I sat up, rubbing my face, I wasn't even conscious of having been asleep.

"What time is it?"

"About two."

My eyeballs were gritty, I was sore all over from riding bareback, and I felt absolutely rotten. "I could sleep for a week."

"Couldn't we all!" Curt said. "I think the horses are rested enough now if we take it a little easy on them. These Indian ponies are tough, though."

We were soon back aboard and at first pushed the ponies to an easy lope for two or three miles, then walked them for about the same distance.

The night seemed to grow darker—if that were possible. I even lost sight of my pony's head, and there was now no question of doing anything but walk. The blackness was so thick I felt I could put out my hand and touch it. We let the ponies pick their own way as best they could in the sooty, predawn blackness, and kept somewhat together by speaking softly to each other every few minutes.

The footing seemed to be getting treacherous; I could feel my pony slipping and catching himself every few steps. He was picking his way as carefully as a mule. I could also hear the hooves squishing and sucking in and out of the mud. I tried to ease my 160 pounds on his back and remain as balanced as possible, but it was difficult without a saddle.

Time passed. I fell into a numb rhythm, rocked by my plodding mount. I gradually forgot everything else. It seemed I had been rocking around on this picket fence of a backbone for an eternity. I dozed, only to be jarred awake when my pony stumbled and I was thrown forward, the stock of the Winchester I had stuck through my belt striking me in the chest.

When I opened my eyes for about the hundredth time, expecting to see only the usual blackness before me, I was surprised to be able to barely make out the outlines of my pony and of those nearby. Very gradually, but steadily, the light increased to finally reveal a soggy, gray dawn and a heavy overcast.

We continued slopping along toward a jagged formation of rugged buttes and rocky spires that jutted up from the rolling grassland several miles ahead of us. It was a landmark to shoot for, but I was glad we hadn't encountered this obstacle in the dead of night.

As if to herald the coming of daylight, it began to rain again, a steady downpour that soaked and chilled to the bone. I glanced around at my companions, who were riding hunched forward, lost in their individual thoughts, looking as miserable as I felt, their hat brims bent down and dripping.

We finally reached the buttes and wound around the bases of these rocky spires in the sticky clay. After twisting and turning around these silent sentinels, we at last emerged on the other side, now sure of our southward direction by the position of the brighter grayness that indicated the long-absent sun.

I could tell by the way I felt and the way my companions looked that we would have to reach food and shelter and rest soon—before we collapsed. Our dash for the Black Hills had turned into a slogging endurance test. For hours we rode, mile after slow mile, in the intermittent rain. Sometimes we dismounted to lead our tired ponies and to give our sore muscles a change. But our boots grew heavy with mud after a few steps, making walking even harder. Every mile or two the grass cover and mud alternated with scrubby patches of cactus.

Late in the afternoon the rain stopped and the day brightened up somewhat. We could see the dark bulk of the Hills looming up many miles ahead, and what we took to be the massive rock of Bear Butte somewhat closer. About an hour before sunset the sun actually popped out of the overcast as the clouds began to break up. The sudden glare almost blinded us. A dark green line of trees that marked a creek ran diagonally across our path about a mile distant.

"Reckon that's another creek or the Belle Fourche?" I wondered aloud.

"Wish I had my map," Wilder said. "Could be Owl Creek. I thought the Belle Fourche ran closer to the Black Hills."

We angled toward the westering sun, our hats tipped over our eyes, and squinted at the line of trees.

"It sure is good to feel the sun again," Cathy remarked, shifting to a more comfortable position on her pony's back. I knew how she felt; my own wet clothes were beginning to itch. But the sun did make things look more cheerful. In spite of my lack of sleep, I began to brighten up and come out of my lethargy.

I think it was Wilder's trained eyes and quick instincts that saved us. His pony was plodding along a little in front and to one side of me. I saw his head jerk up and he started to rein in, but he almost instantly checked himself and kept the pony walking. "There's an Indian on horseback in those trees," he said quietly to us, turning his head slightly. "Don't let on there's anything wrong. Could be a party of Sioux or Cheyenne." A few seconds of tense silence followed.

"What now?" Wiley Jenkins asked, his voice apprehensive.

Wilder didn't answer right away. I'm sure he was weighing our options. They seemed few. There was virtually no place to hide, and to turn and run would have alerted them that they had been spotted. Our tired ponies would be no match for their mounts. But to keep riding might very shortly put us right into an ambush.

Under the brim of my hat, my eyes swept the line of trees, alert to any movement or sign of life. But I could pick out nothing.

"Don't see him now," Wilder said quietly. "But I'm sure I saw him. And if there's one, they're bound to be more. They seldom travel solo in hostile territory."

The ponies clopped along in the heavy, oppressive silence, each step bringing us closer to the vengeance of the Sioux in the form of arrow, lance, or bullet. Prickly fingers of fear began to crawl up my back. My worst fears were realized. Caught in the open in daylight! Had we tempted fate in the form of hostile Sioux or Cheyenne too long? Were we to survive battles and scouting parties and skirmishes all summer, only to be cut down, defenseless, by a roaming war party?

In spite of my anxiety, I smiled ruefully at the thought of how puzzled the Indians must be to see four whites riding toward them, bareback, on Indian ponies—and especially to see one of the hated bluecoats riding one of their own mounts.

"Anybody has any ideas, now's the time to spit 'em out," Curt Wilder said.

Nobody spoke.

"Okay, then, here's my plan." He spoke tersely. "The sun lacks about a half hour of setting. If we can somehow stall that long without rousing their suspicions, we may have a chance in the dark. Now, very gradually, turn your ponies to the right, like we're going to parallel the stream for a ways, looking for a camping site. That will keep us somewhat out of range for now and, the way the creek is coming toward us, it'll take us at a widening angle from that line of trees. And spread out abreast so we'll make a smaller target from where they're looking."

We nudged our ponies and did as we were told, making a wide turn. When we were finally riding parallel and slightly away from the creek, I had trouble keeping my eyes away from the silent green line of foliage that held the unseen watchers. I had the feeling that if I looked away, I would suddenly feel a bullet slam into my unprotected flesh. I hadn't felt this helpless since two months before, when we had been trapped in the Big Horns.

Trying to appear casual, I took off my hat and swung it vigorously to shake out some of the wet, meantime taking a look at the September sun that was showing as a red disk through the haze in the western sky. It moved with an agonizing slowness.

Suddenly, Curt pulled up his pony and slid off its back. Handing me the reins, he bent and picked up his pony's left forefoot and made as if to examine it. "Just killing time," he said quietly. We all dismounted and crowded around and pretended to discuss the problem.

"How many shells have you got for that Winchester, Matt?"

"Seven in the magazine and—" I slipped my fingers unobtrusively along the cartridge loops in my belt. "—ten more. And four in my Colt, I think. About twenty-one, all told."

"Anybody else have a gun?" Curt inquired, still rubbing dirt from the pony's hoof.

The other two shook their heads. Wiley Jenkins, who

hated violence, had not even owned a gun, and Cathy's heavy Colt had been left behind in the excitement of the escape.

"Two guns and twenty-one shots among the four of us," Curt said. "It'll have to do." Luckily, the shells for my octagon-barreled Winchester '73 and my Colt were interchangeable.

I took off my hat and wiped a damp sleeve across my forehead, glancing toward the west as I did so. The sun had dropped behind the trees, and long shadows were streaking the plains.

We managed to kill a few more minutes as Curt dropped his pony's forefoot and picked up the other, studying the tree line from under the animal's belly. "This won't work much longer," Curt said. "If they want us, they'll be out to get us before dark. They'd much rather take us by surprise, but if we don't walk into their trap, they'll probably try something else. Matt, slip me your Colt and a few shells. Keep the rifle; you're a better shot than any of us with that. If we have to make a break for it, keep together and ride like hell toward the trees." Squatting on his haunches, he glanced up at us and smiled grimly. "Any of you too tired to make it?"

We all shook our heads silently. Wiley and I were gaunt, red-eyed, and unshaven. Cathy's healthy beauty had deteriorated. Her uncombed brown hair clung damply to her pale forehead. Dark circles held her brownish-green eyes. We had lived and slept in our wet clothes for many days, and were all short on food and sleep. We had had nothing to eat or drink in the past twenty-four hours except some dirty rainwater. But, wan and forlorn as we looked in our mud-spattered fatigue, I knew the tension was giving us an energy we didn't really possess. Our lives were on the line, and we weren't about to give them up without a fight, especially after what we had already been through.

I, for one, was almost eager for some kind of confrontation or flight—any kind of action to relieve the unbearable tension. I didn't have long to wait.

Two of our ponies, standing docile and tired, suddenly jerked up their heads as a slight evening breeze brought the scent of the Indians or their horses. One of our mounts whinnied. Sensing their element of surprise was gone, the war party instantly burst from the cover of the trees and, yelling wildly, rode straight for us.

CHAPTER 2

As though we were all shot from the same cannon, the four of us sprang as one to the backs of our ponies and dug our heels into their flanks. The ponies lunged away with renewed energy. We angled away from the Indians and toward the trees, riding hard. Out of the corner of my eye I saw the painted and feathered riders turn to head us off. I heard a couple of shots fired but paid no mind, since most Indians are notoriously poor shots, and it would have taken a mighty lucky shot or an expert marksman from a stable position to hit a moving target at this distance in the half-light.

Our lives literally depended on our reaching shelter first, with a few seconds to get ready to defend. But it looked as though they had the angle on us and would be on us before we could reach the trees. A shallow wash several yards wide suddenly loomed up under our ponies' hooves in the dusk. We had no time to turn, but rode right down through a spray of muddy water, our momentum carrying us up the other side and out.

The wash grew narrower and deeper as it neared the creek it fed, and the war party hit it some two hundred yards farther down. In their rush to head us off, the first few of the dozen or so riders were on it before they saw it, and tried to jump their ponies. The first two barely made it, their mounts almost falling as the ponies clawed for a foothold in the opposite muddy bank. Three more behind them, unable to check their rush or to jump clear of the forerunners, fell in a tangle of legs into the wash, throwing their riders. The rest of the Indians, expert horsemen that they were, turned their ponies sharply or brought them to a sliding stop, short of the declivity.

I saw all of this in two quick glances as we rode hell-bent for cover.

This fortunate accident gave us the moment or so we needed to outrun them. Curt and Cathy hit the cotton-woods and willows first, Wiley and I only a couple of seconds behind. It was even darker under the trees, and we plunged blindly through, our ponies flopping about three feet down the bank into the water of the creek. The shock of the cold water took my breath as I was thrown and went under, trying instinctively to keep a hold on my pony's hackamore. The current was swift, but the creek was only three to four feet deep with a gravel bottom. My mount jerked free and plunged away as I floundered to my feet.

"You two get downstream—fast!" Curt yelled. "Matt and I'll hold 'em off."

I yanked the rifle from my belt as the two of us struggled to shore. We scrambled up under the trees, shaking the water from our weapons.

"Thank God for sealed cartridges," Curt panted.

"Amen to that!"

We threw ourselves belly-down at the base of a huge cottonwood tree, and I levered a shell into the chamber. The war party had gotten itself together, with the exception of two I could see on foot in the distance. The rest were pounding toward us, whooping.

I knew they couldn't see us in the gathering dusk under the trees, but they knew where we had gone in and they were closing in for the kill—or capture. But the way they were streaked and daubed with paint, I didn't think they were in any mood to take prisoners, unless they had a little entertaining torture in mind.

Curt had loaded my Colt before they jumped us, and I had crammed my magazine full as well, before we divided up the remaining shells. "Hold until you're sure of your first shot," Curt ordered. "You take one of 'em on the left and I'll take one on the right."

My heart was pounding so hard I thought it would

jump out of my chest, and not just from exertion. As I propped my left elbow and sighted, my hands shook. Out of the corner of my eyes, I could see Curt bracing the revolver with both hands.

The ten riders were within sixty yards now, the feathers flying from their long black hair and from the tips of their repeating rifles. Damn the man who ever sold them such weapons! I thought, lining up a brave in my sights and drawing a long breath.

Fifty yards, forty yards, thirty yards . . .

"Now!" Curt's voice was low and very clear.

Our guns roared as one. Two riders jerked and spun limply from their ponies. Before they hit the ground I had thrown the lever on my rifle and was squeezing off another shot. But I was too hasty, and missed. Cursing myself, I slammed another cartridge into the chamber. Before I could fire again, the band broke apart and began to spread out in either direction.

A pony suddenly went down, shot by Curt. The thrown rider was just rolling to his feet when the six-shooter roared again and the Sioux went down for good.

I fired again and saw one rider grab his arm as his pony swerved away. The attack was faltering. I fired twice more and missed. It was getting dark fast, and the moving targets were getting harder to hit. And the Sioux were now hanging to the offsides of their ponies, firing at us from under the ponies' necks. It was an exhibition of equestrian skill I had been before, but still marveled at. The Plains Indians were very likely the best horsemen in the world. But I had no time to contemplate this theory. Bullets were whizzing over my head, ripping through the leaves. One or two lucky shots kicked rough bark from the cottonwood trunk a couple of feet from our heads.

I wormed my way forward to the edge of the under-growth and strained to see if any of the attackers were trying to get into the tree line above or below us. But I couldn't see where most of them had gone. We had killed or disabled three and wounded one that I knew of. Three were afoot from their horses falling into the wash. Just then, I saw three of the Indians riding back to pick up their walking companions.

I pumped three more shots in the direction of the moving horsemen, but it was now so dark I would never know if I had hit anything.

There was no answering fire.

"Come on, Matt." Curt's voice was low, a few feet behind me. "We've stung 'em pretty good. Let's get out of here while they're recouping." He was a man whom crisis made quiet. I didn't need any urging. Scrambling back, we waded into the stream, holding our weapons out of the water.

"Think they're slipping around to head us off?" I asked. "They sure disappeared quick."

"Maybe, but I doubt it. They don't like to fight in the dark. They'll probably collect their dead and retreat for now. We got at least three of them and wounded another. Those three who were afoot were temporarily out of action. They paid a high price for not getting at least one of us. By my count, that left only about five mounted warriors."

We were wading toward the middle of the stream, and the current tore at us, making it hard to keep our footing on the smooth pebbles and hard-packed clay bottom as the water rose above our waists. The stream was about a hundred feet wide, as near as I could judge. I couldn't see or hear anything of our ponies.

"Where'd Wiley and Cathy go?" I whispered hoarsely.

"Don't know. Hope they got downstream fast and far." He moved closer to me in the dark and spoke softly, even though the sound of rushing water probably drowned his voice from anyone on the bank. "Let's swim with this current—quietly. Cathy and Wiley can't be far ahead of us. And they may still have the ponies."

We were pretty well toward the middle of the stream by this time, and I was taking one last look around at the blackness when a Winchester exploded not twenty yards away and I felt the bullet yank at the sleeve of my shirt. My heart jumped, and I instinctively raised my rifle to fire, but Curt, always quick-thinking, grabbed the barrel and hissed into my ear. "No! They'll see the flash. Pretend we're hit. Let's go!"

He gave a realistic, agonized yell and splashed around, at the same time pulling me down and away into the current. I managed to jam the rifle back into my belt and pushed off the bottom into an easy sidestroke, swimming quietly with my eyes and nose barely above the surface, letting the cold, swift water do most of the work.

We swam this way for at least ten minutes, and no more shots came from the darkness. The lone rifle blast may have been a parting shot from some brave who had tried to slip up and count coup on us, not knowing we were already in the river. I don't know how he could have spotted us except, possibly, by our white faces and hands. Or else he just heard a little noise and fired at it. I prayed that these Sioux had a strong belief in the afterlife, especially in the notion that their souls would wander forever without rest and never find their way to happiness if they were killed in the darkness. My imagination peopled the blackness of the shoreline with countless savages, all thirsting for my blood. I urged my arms and legs to swim a little faster.

I estimated that the current was ripping along at a good five miles per hour. I was so keyed up it was difficult to judge time, but I guessed we swam this way for at least thirty minutes, even though it seemed like hours. That would put us about two miles downstream from where we went into the river. The ten-pound rifle was beginning to become bothersome, stuck through my belt, but I wouldn't have parted from its reassuring weight for anything.

Curt was swimming slightly ahead of me, and without warning, he put his feet down and stood up. I piled into him, and we went down again splashing. We both floundered to our feet and stood there, the current sucking and gurgling around us.

"What's wrong?" I asked in a whisper.

"You see something over there near the bank?"

I strained my eyes and saw what looked like an irregular white spot, but I had no idea what it was. Even as I looked, the spot moved. My heart jumped.

"I think it's one of our ponies, standing in the water under the overhang," Curt said quietly, his mouth close to my ear. "One of ours had a white marking just back of the shoulders. I'm going to take a chance. Be ready to get underwater and swim hard." Then he moved away from me, and in a strong but guarded voice, called, "Wiley! Cathy!" There was no immediate answer, and I was ready to spring away. "Wiley! Cathy!" he called a little louder.

"Curt?" came a tentative query.

My breath came whistling out in an involuntary sigh as I recognized Wiley's voice. In a few seconds we were all reunited. They had managed to hang on to two of our four ponies. Since Curt didn't think we were out of danger yet, we walked, leading our ponies downstream another mile or so, keeping to the edge of the tree line on the south shore, opposite the side of the attack. Finally, he called a halt.

"Think this is far enough?"

"I wouldn't be satisfied until we were twenty or thirty miles away, but this'll have to do."

He led the ponies into a dense thicket of trees and undergrowth. A rising three-quarter moon cast a pale, patchy light on the leaves and revealed an open, grassy area between the brush and the riverbank.

"We'll camp here. We're all done in. We'd never make it if we tried to go any farther tonight. And I don't want daylight to catch us out in the open again like it did today. It wasn't our vigilance that saved us. We were just damned lucky. We'll have to be more careful from here on."

He looked around at us in the dark. Curt and I had lost our hats. The four of us were soaked and chilled to the bone. We were half dead on our feet from hunger and exhaustion.

"We'll have to have food," Curt said, as if thinking aloud.

"Hell, we haven't seen as much as a jackrabbit since we left Slim Buttes," Wiley Jenkins said. "Only sign of life I saw the whole way was a couple of buzzards and a hawk."

"How about some pony steaks?" I suggested.

"Just what I was thinking," Curt agreed. "We can walk to the Hills from here. I hate to lose one of our two remaining mounts, but we'll never make it, even with horses, if we don't get something to eat. Which one of these two is the weaker?"

"This one," Wiley answered.

"A bullet will be the quickest and most humane way," Curt Wilder said. When no one moved, he apparently interpreted this as a reluctance on our part to kill the animal, although I was just numb with fatigue. "I'll do it," he continued. "We'll just have to risk the Indians' hearing a shot. I think I can muffle it. We don't have a club or a knife big enough to do the job."

Without further hesitation, he took the reins of the weaker animal and led him away downriver. The rest of us stood there not saying a word. A few minutes later we heard a muffled boom, which I'm sure could not have been heard over a half-mile away, especially with the noise of the rushing water nearby.

I shook myself out of my lethargy and went to help him carve the meat with Wiley's short sheath knife. "We going to eat this raw?" I asked as we carried the steaks back to Wiley and Cathy.

"I've got some wax-coated matches I've been carrying for weeks," he answered. "Hope we can find something dry enough to burn."

We found some dead grass and leaves and enough twigs and driftwood to kindle a small fire. We fed the minute flame with sprigs of grass and tiny twigs. When the fire eventually began to feed on itself, the wood sizzled as the water boiled out. We took pains to build it in the midst of the thickest part of the damp undergrowth where it would not be visible, and made it only large enough to cook on. We whittled some forked green sticks and roasted the steaks over the fire. And even though we had no salt, no bread, no vegetables, nor coffee to go with it, I believe that was the most delicious meal I have ever eaten. It may have been my extreme hunger, but that pony meat surpassed in taste the best beef I'd ever had.

"By golly, my hat's off to you, Matt Tierney," Curt said, giving me a whiskery grin across the campfire.

"Why's that?" I asked, cutting off another bite of the tender, succulent pony meat and popping it between my teeth.

"When the chips are down in a fight, I'll vote to have an Irishman on my side every time. You're a native son, born and reared, and you proved it just now."

"Aw, c'mon, now," I answered. "Everybody seems to have that image of us, just because we've been fighting off the damn English for a few hundred years. Actually, Ireland is known as the 'Land of Saints and Scholars.' "

"It's also known as the land of boozers and brawlers," Curt said, a twinkle in his bloodshot eyes. "And I'm glad to say it was the brawler part that was showing just now, or we probably wouldn't be sitting here eating and resting."

"I believe you've kissed the Blarney stone a time or two," I retorted, feeling my face reddening at his praise. "Actually, it was your sharp eye that kept us from walking into that ambush."

When we had all eaten as much as our shrunken stomachs would hold, we took turns wringing out our soaked clothing and attempting to dry it by propping our shirts on sticks near the flames. The wet cloth served as something of a screen and helped to create a small circle of steaming warmth.

Curt and I each had a watch, but both of them had stopped after their soak in the river. I judged it was about midnight before we roasted a little more of the meat and ate again.

I was using my half-dry shirttail to wipe off the breech of my rifle when Cathy stifled a yawn. A few seconds later her brother yawned mightily. Across the dying fire the conversation had lagged, and I noticed Curt's eyelids drooping. The food, the warmth, the relaxation of the tension, and the nearly two days with little sleep were doing their work.

"Think we need to post a guard?" I asked.

"Think any one of us could stay awake for more than ten minutes without someone to talk to?" Curt countered.

"You're right," I said, grinning.

"I think we ought to picket that pony about fifty yards away in the dense brush. He might give us a warning if we need one. Frankly, if I know anything about the Sioux and Cheyenne, we won't be bothered again tonight. I think that was a chance meeting. They may have been on their way to join Crazy Horse in harassing the troops."

He began scraping dirt on the remainder of our glowing fire. "Just be sure to sleep with your gun handy. How many shells have you got left? Let's divvy up." We counted out ten, divided them equally, and loaded our weapons.

Wiley took the pony some fifty yards upstream and tethered him so he could graze out of sight along the timbered bank, then came back and we all rolled near each other on the ground and were dead to the world instantly. The whole Sioux nation could have come in yelling and screaming, and I probably wouldn't have awakened, I was so tired. Divine providence must have been watching over us that night, because we were not discovered or disturbed. In fact, my exhaustion was so complete and I slept so soundly that I didn't even dream, which was unusual.

When I finally woke, I immediately tensed and slid my hand for the reassuring feel of my rifle. My hand closed on its cool metal on the ground about two feet from where I lay on my back. My irritated eyes were nearly stuck shut, and I couldn't see until I wiped them open with my other hand. I could feel the sun warming me here and there as it filtered through the foliage. I thought I heard the wind blowing, but as I rolled over and looked around, I realized it was only the rushing sound of the river a few yards away.

Curt was awake and sitting a few feet off, watching me. Wiley and Cathy were still asleep, lying huddled on the ground on the other side of our cold campfire.

"Morning," Curt greeted in a low voice. "Sorry I haven't got any coffee to offer you," he said with a grin.

"I sure could use some," I groaned, sitting up and stretching. "I feel like I've been run over by a team of oxen. Any sign of the hostiles?"

"None. But I think we should stay here and rest up today and travel at night."

"Yeah. I'm still dead tired." I glanced over at him. "And you don't look too pert yourself." His lean cheeks were covered by several days' worth of dark stubble, even though his eyes looked a little more rested and clear. He sat cross-legged on the ground, resting his elbows on his knees. His boots were coated with dried mud. In spite of our swim, the yellow cavalry stripes on the outside of his trouser legs were all but obliterated by weeks of grime and mud. His cavalry jacket was missing two or three buttons and had a ragged bullet hole in one sleeve where he had wrapped the muzzle of my Colt before shooting the pony. I noticed that his captain's shoulder bars were missing. Apparently, Major Zimmer had had them torn off when Curt was arrested and confined, even though, from what little I knew of army regulations, I thought this was technically illegal until a man was convicted. Or, for that matter, Curt might have done it himself, later. But I didn't want to bring up a sore subject, so I just said, indicating Cathy and Wiley, "I'm glad they're sleeping; they needed it."

"They sure did."

"How long have you been awake?"

"An hour or so, I guess."

A movement in the trees and a flash of color upstream caught my eye, and I jerked my Winchester up, my heart skipping a beat.

"Relax. It's just our pony. I checked on him earlier. He's all right."

I stretched again and yawned, my heartbeat beginning to slow down after the sudden fright. I laid the rifle on the ground and stood up, feeling stiff and rusty.

"Have a wash in the river. It'll freshen you up."

"Good idea."

I went to the edge of the stream and splashed some of the icy water on my face, scrubbing it in vigorously and feeling the tingle. When I came back, dripping and running my fingers through the tangle of my hair, Curt was busy gathering some dry twigs to resurrect our small fire.

"Whew! That'll wake you up," I said. "What about the smoke from our fire? Aren't you afraid it'll be seen?"

"Not if we keep it small—just big enough to cook on. What little smoke it makes will be dissipated by these overhead trees."

When the fire began to blaze up from its hidden embers, I retrieved the meat we had slung from a halter in a nearby willow tree. The flies had already found it, but we were in no position to be squeamish.

Our breakfast was sizzling over the low flames before Cathy and Wiley awakened.

"Man, that smells good!" Wiley said, sitting up and looking around, obviously not quite sure where he was.

Cathy came awake quietly and completely in just a few seconds. She sat up, composed and ladylike, pushing her short hair back from her face, and reached for a piece of the roasted pony meat Curt handed her on a green twig. Even in her bedraggled condition, she was very pretty. As I watched her, I couldn't decide if this was because of her youth or if she had the bone structure and the classic type of beauty that would endure for years. In any case, she was Curt's girl, and I wasn't likely to be around twenty years from now to find out. In fact, none of the four of us might survive to middle age.

After we had eaten our fill again, Curt and I walked the hundred yards or so to the carcass of the butchered pony in the trees along the river downstream.

I was glad I had already eaten, or I probably would have lost my appetite. The bloody carcass was anything but inviting. Four black and white magpies and a big golden eagle flapped away as we came up. We carved some more meat from the hindquarters and carried it back to camp. Curt sharpened Wiley's knife on a rock and spent the next hour or two cutting the meat into thin strips and grilling it well-done over the fire.

"We won't be here long enough to smoke this stuff to make it keep. We should be in the Black Hills in short order, and it should stay good as long as we'll need it. I hope so, anyway."

Cathy excused herself and told us she was going for a bath in the river.

"Don't worry if I'm not back in a jiffy," she told us. "Now that I feel like I might live again, I'm going to get myself good and clean, and also see if I can wash these clothes. Then I'm going to find a good sunny spot and get everything good and dry. I've been wet so long, I may never get my skin unwrinkled."

"It would be tough to explain to people that I have a sister who is permanently pruned up," Wiley said, grinning. "Don't go far," he cautioned her.

"Okay. I'm just going up to about where the pony is tied. Sure wish I had some soap and a hairbrush."

"If wishes were carriages, we could all ride into Deadwood in style," her brother reminded her.

"Guess you're right," she sighed, moving off.

The rest of the day was spent resting, dozing, and eating. Every hour or so Curt and I would cautiously venture out from the tree line, keeping low in the grass, and survey the terrain as far as we could see, to guard against any surprises. We would also strip off our dry clothes and wade across the river to do the same thing on the opposite side. There were no good climbing trees in the vicinity, or we could have gotten a better view of the countryside. The willows were too small, and the cottonwoods were too large—with no limbs low enough on their huge trunks to be reached.

I slept again for about two hours in the late afternoon, and the others did the same at different times. Our fatigue was deep-seated. Even though I had always heard that older people didn't need as much sleep as younger ones, Curt and I seemed to need as much rest as Wiley—who was only about twenty-six and Cathy, who was only twenty-one. Curt and I were both in our early thirties. But maybe this phenomenon didn't show itself until a person reached his late fifties or sixties. By sundown, I, for one, felt pretty well rested.

"How far do we have to go?" Wiley asked, directing his question to no one in particular as the four of us sat around our fire at sunset eating more of the pony meat.

"If this is the Belle Fourche River, and I think it is," Curt replied, automatically assuming his place as leader, "then I'd guess we've got about twenty miles to the Hills proper, and then maybe another ten to Deadwood. We had Bear Butte in sight before the attack last night, so if we get out of this little valley before total darkness sets in, we should be able to guide on it. We should be almost due northeast from Deadwood."

Even though we were all getting tired of the same diet, we were glad to have it. Monotonous it may have been, but nourishing and strengthening it certainly was. We stuffed down as much of it as we could hold, knowing we would need the energy for the long night of walking ahead.

Just as dusk was fading into night, we gathered ourselves together and set out, Cathy taking the first turn on the pony and the rest of us walking. The moon gave us its light as we plodded along, hour after hour, in a general southwest direction. Since none of our watches was working, we could only guess at the time by the position of the moon. We took turns riding the pony and walking, and—with our dry clothes, food, and rest—we all felt a hundred percent better than we had felt after we made our escape from Slim Buttes.

Sometime after midnight we came off the rolling prairie and entered some low hills. The fresh scent of pine greeted our noses. The hills gradually grew steeper and higher, and we had to pause more often to get our bearings and be sure we were still headed in the right direction. Then, in the wee hours of the morning, the moon went down and we had to stop, knowing that we were likely to walk off some steep drop-off in the rugged, rocky hills. The darkness enveloped us like a velvety black curtain. The only stars that could be seen were directly overhead between the tall conifers.

We tied the pony to a small tree and we all sat down to rest and await the coming of daylight. Now that we had the hills and trees around us, we all felt more secure, even though the danger from Indians was not past. At least there were more places to hide.

On a soft carpet of pine needles, I dozed, then slept. When I woke, another clear dawn was just breaking. The others were already awake, and we started out again, after chewing on some of the well-cooked pony meat Curt had packed. Traveling the ridges of the hills as much as possible, we soon sighted what looked like a raw mining camp below us in a canyon.

"If that's Crook City, then we're on course," Curt said. "I was talking to some of the miners who were with the cavalry, and they told me it was just a few miles down the same canyon from Deadwood."

We pushed on, following the ridge. We could see miners working their sluice boxes in the creeks below us as we went along. The gulch was ripped and torn by picks and shovels all up and down both sides. Here and there, in odd places, we saw small piles of white quartz, looking like snow, where it had been dumped by the prospectors.

By late morning we spotted what had to be the new town of Deadwood ahead of us through the trees. We stopped on the crest of the hill and looked down.

'Well, there she is," Curt said. "It's got to be Deadwood."

Cathy slid off the pony's back and came up to stand by his side.

"I wonder what's waitin' for us there?" Wiley said, as if thinking aloud.

"Whatever it is," Wiley said, "we've beaten the army to it by at least twenty-four hours."

CHAPTER 3

With the end of our marathon in sight, the fatigue and danger of the past few days faded like a bad dream.

"Deadwood Gulch! By God!" Wiley exclaimed aloud more than once as he led the pony down the steep hillside through the birch and fir trees toward the ramshackle settlement.

After he had said this for about the third time, Cathy said, "Wiley, you sound like you're looking at the pot of gold at the end of the rainbow, instead of a raw mining town."

A grin cracked his handsome face—the old, familiar, boyish grin we hadn't seen in several days. "I've lowered my sights some. Anything that smacks of civilization would look like heaven compared to what we've seen since Cheyenne last spring. Besides, from what I've heard about the gold around here, this may *be* the pot at the end of the rainbow."

"Hold up a minute." Wilder stopped us. "Give me your knife, Wiley."

Curt proceeded to slit the stitching from the top of the yellow facings on his trouser legs. Then he ripped the stripes down and off. He cut the remaining brass buttons from his tunic and took a look to make sure no more identifiable markings of the army uniform were still visible. He had no hat. He removed his jacket, rolled it up, and handed it to Wiley.

"If we're going to walk in there in broad daylight, I don't want any questions asked about me being with the army. A lot of ex-soldiers wear pieces of uniforms, so we probably won't be noticed."

24

When we finally reached the bottom of the gulch and came up on the lower end of the town, I could see what a really raw camp it was. As we ambled slowly up the street leading the pony, I'm sure our stares compared to those of some country hicks seeing a big city for the first time. Cathy, in the travels with her late father, had probably seen more of these frontier boom towns than any of us. As for me, it was the first time I had ever been in a mining camp during the first few months of its existence. And the impression was one of chaos. People were swarming everywhere, like bees in a hive. Mostly there were muddy, bearded miners, with merchants, bullwhackers, and men of every description thrown in. And men were all I saw; not a woman was in sight.

Two long, twelve-oxen bull trains with tandem wagons had apparently just pulled in with several tons of freight and were half turned, blocking the entire upper end of the winding, hard-packed dirt street. Two wagon drivers were yelling and cursing the bullwhackers to move their teams. The street itself was fifteen to twenty yards wide and it curved back and forth, following the bottom of the gulch. The thoroughfare was jammed with buckboards, Studebaker wagons, piles of fresh lumber, men on horseback and afoot.

There was a sawmill somewhere in the vicinity. I could hear the protesting whine of saws ripping lumber over the general din of voices, mules braying, hammers banging, harness jingling, the hollow thudding of boots on boardwalks, and a cacophony of other sounds. The main and only street of town was lined with wooden buildings, and the sides of the gulch that sloped steeply up behind each of these rows of structures had been almost denuded of trees to build the town, leaving thousands of stumps on the barren hillsides. The lower end of the street contained some large, white-walled tents set on log foundations. The rough spruce, pine, and fir boards that formed the fronts of the unpainted buildings were still oozing sap. The more pretentious establishments were two storied and sported coats of paint, and even cornices and brick chimneys. They also had glass windows and, amazingly enough, even had the appearance of permanence. Considering that nearly everything except the wood had to be freighted in by wagon over many miles of very rough roads—through hostile territory from Cheyenne to the south or Pierre to the east—I was astonished at how all of this could have sprung out of the virgin wilderness in a matter of only a few months. It was all a monument to the glittering yellow metal the white man coveted. I could see signs advertising a bakery, two dry-goods stores, two hotels, a bank, a telegraph office, two or three restaurants, a couple of grocery stores, and a large stagecoach office and stable. Some enterprising dentist had even hung out his shingle in this remote frontier town.

It seemed every second or third building we passed was a saloon or liquor dealer.

"A man with cash sure wouldn't go thirsty here," Wiley remarked, licking his lips as though he were already tasting his first drink in weeks. Loud arguments drifted to our ears over the bat-wing doors of one saloon as we went by. A crash of glass, some yells, and a splintering of wood in another one told of a real disagreement in progress. Things were in full swing, and it wasn't yet noon.

The sun was directly overhead and beating down into the windless gulch, bringing out the smells of manure and pine resin. I was beginning to sweat under my ragged corduroy jacket. But it was a pleasant feeling after being cold and wet for more than a month.

"Well, what do we get first?" I asked. "Food, drink, bath, or bed?"

"All. And in about that order, for me anyway," Cathy replied, sliding her hat back to let it hang by its cord from her neck and tossing her head to shake her hair loose. It fell just to the collar of her doeskin jacket.

Several men on the sidewalk nearby just then noticed that Cathy was a woman and stopped their conversation to stare in our direction.

"Stay close," Curt told her quietly. "I have a feeling women are pretty scarce in this town—decent women anyway."

"How much money have we got?" Wiley asked. "Cathy

and I have about one hundred and thirty dollars Dad had when he was killed." He was matter-of-fact, giving no indication that he was still being torn by guilt and grief from the death of his father at the Battle of the Rosebud back in June.

"Well, I think I've got nearly three months' pay," Curt said, digging into a side pocket. "They didn't bother to take anything but my side arms from me when I was arrested." He pulled out a damp leather billfold and counted out something over four hundred dollars.

"Looks like I'm low man on this money tree," I grinned, holding up two bills. "Thirty dollars. I worked all summer for the *Chicago Times Herald*, and then decided to skip out without going back East for my pay."

"Don't worry. We've got plenty for the four of us for the time," Curt said. "Why don't we all go get a good bath, then some food and some new clothes? And no drinking until we're settled in," he added as he noticed Wiley tying up the Indian pony to a hitching rail and eyeing the Union Brewery Saloon just across the boardwalk.

Wiley's amiable expression froze and he started to make some retort, but checked himself. In a moment he relaxed and snorted gently. "Yeah, I guess you're right. I can be thirsty a little longer."

We turned the pony into a livery stable and then turned ourselves into a barber shop that advertised a bathhouse in the rear section. We all soaked and scrubbed and luxuriated in the hot, soapy water for some three-quarters of an hour. One small section of the room with one tub had been partitioned off for the use of any infrequent women customers, so Cathy was able to enjoy complete privacy. It was the first real bath any of us had had since early summer. When we finally climbed out of the wooden tubs and dressed, we three men went out front into the tonsorial parlor and got shaved and our hair cut while Cathy waited for us. Wiley kept his sand-colored mustache. It did give his youthful face a slightly more mature look, even though the mustache was several shades lighter than his wavy brown hair.

"Hell, Wiley, I can't even see it from here," Curt chided him, backing away about twenty feet.

Even though we had to put our old, dirty, ragged clothes back on, we came out feeling renewed and refreshed. We wore the clothes only long enough to get down the street to a store that advertised Hobson's General Merchandise. And general it was: light and heavy clothing, hardware, tinware, mess pans, camp kettles, harness, saddlery, blankets, india rubber boots, ponchos, garden seeds, canned and dried fruits, sardines and yeast powders, lanterns and nails. There were goods of all kinds crammed into every corner and hung from all the walls. Bigger equipment hung from large hooks embedded in the ceiling beams. There was hardly room to walk among the piles and stacks and shelves of merchandise. Apparently, the storekeeper had just received a shipment or two and he was stocking up for the winter.

Deciding what to buy was no problem; finding the right size was, at least for Cathy. She was finally able to find a man's small shirt and a pair of canvas pants that fit her fairly well, as well as a pair of long cotton underwear.

Nowhere in town, the lanky clerk told us, did he know of any place that stocked women's underclothes. There was simply no demand for them as yet.

"I assume," he said, his face reddening slightly, "that the girls at Myra's Golden Bell brought their own."

"Myra's Golden Bell?" Wiley asked.

"It . . . it's a place—uh, sort of like a red-light house down on the lower end of Main Street," he answered, trying to keep Cathy from overhearing. "It's a saloon on the first floor."

"I see."

We all outfitted ourselves from the skin out, buying stiff new overall pants and plaid wool shirts. We also picked up some soft corduroy pants. Curt and I replaced our lost hats with two low-crowned felts with brims of medium width. The stock of clothing was plentiful, but not too varied in styles. Our boots had been soaked and dried so often that they were shrunken and falling apart. We replaced them with low-heeled, round-toed leather boots similar to the standard issue cavalry boot, except that these had shorter tops. Again, Cathy had difficulty finding some small enough, but after much searching, the blushing young clerk finally fitted her with a pair that she could wear. The whole time he was helping her slip the boots off and on, he was casting admiring glances at her.

Before paying for our new outfits and leaving, we also stocked up on such items as combs, handkerchiefs, and socks. We were even able to find toothbrushes. As we pulled out our greenbacks to pay, the clerk's eyes opened wide. "You must be new in town," he said.

"Sure. Isn't everybody?"

"I mean, real new. You've got paper money. You get five-percent discount on all our merchandise for this."

"For what?"

"Everybody in town, including the bank, will give you five percent more for this in gold than its face value."

Our faces must have registered a blankness, because he went on. "Paper money is scarce here, but it's more valuable because it's lighter and easier to carry around than gold dust or nuggets."

He pulled out a soft buckskin bag with a drawstring and went around behind the counter to the delicate balance scales and carefully sifted out our change. "You got anything to carry this in?" We shook our heads. "Here, this is on the house." He tossed a small buckskin bag, similar to his own, on the counter.

"Thanks."

We came back out into the bright sunshine and started down the street.

"Let's get a hotel room and go for some food," Curt suggested. This time Wiley agreed readily.

"How about that one?" I pointed to a wooden building across the street.

"The Merchants Hotel. Now that's an original name," Wiley remarked dryly as we picked our way among the wagons and mules to cross the street.

We rented two adjacent rooms on the second floor. Curt specified that we get front rooms, overlooking Main Street. Cathy's room was on the corner and ours was in the center of the building. The roof, which formed one wall of Cathy's room, sloped inward, but despite this awkward feature, the room was plenty spacious. The bedsteads were of wood, apparently homemade and hastily knocked together. There was one crude wooden chair in each room and an empty hogshead that served as the only table. This table held a coal-oil lamp and a tin basin and pitcher. In place of closets, three wooden pegs were affixed to a wall in each room. The unpainted board walls still smelled pleasantly of pine resin.

"I'll bet this place is mighty cold in the winer," Curt remarked as we stood in Cathy's room looking around at the unsealed walls and noting the lack of any type of stove.

"Maybe you're just supposed to wrap yourself in that," Wiley said, pointing at the thick feather tick on the bed.

"Let's get some extra blankets," Curt said. "Our room has only one bed, too, so somebody'll be sleeping on the floor."

"At least there's a rug covering part of the floor."

"Yeah, I'll bet it's really clean," Wiley said with a grimace.

"For somebody who's been sleeping in tents and on the muddy ground for weeks, you're mighty particular," his sister shot back.

The one practical amenity that softened the appearance of the two rooms were some gauzy-looking curtains at the windows.

The desk clerk recommended the Grand Central Hotel Restaurant as a good place to eat. "They're not really my competitor, since we don't serve food here," he explained.

Within the hour we were seated in the commodious dining room of the Grand Central, about a block away, enjoying a meal of elk steaks, fried potatoes, corn, peas, brown bread, coffee, and stewed apples. To our way of thinking, it was a feast fit for royalty. And nobody better deserving of it than ourselves.

Since it was midafternoon, there were only a few other

patrons in the place. Once the waiter had brought our
food, he disappeared—except when called for an occasional refill—and left us free to talk without being
overheard.

"Well, what do we do now?" Wiley asked, pushing his
chair back from the table, crossing his legs, and lighting a
long, slim cigar. "We could probably get out of here and
head on down to Cheyenne if we can get some horses, or
if there's a stage line out of here."

"There's nothing in Cheyenne I want to see," I answered.
"Speaking for myself, I'd like to stick around here for a
few days to see what's going on. But I'll have to get myself
a grubstake. From what I've seen of the prices here, my
thirty dollars won't last past tomorrow."

"Well, you know what's mine is yours," Curt answered.
"If it hadn't been for the three of you, I'd be facing a
court-martial right about now."

"Would that be any worse than being branded a deserter?" I asked.

"Yes. I'd have had the disgrace of a publicized trial
and probably a dishonorable discharge from the service.
And there was a good chance I'd have been sentenced to
a term at that new federal prison at Leavenworth."

"But you were an officer."

"Just so. And the senior court officers would have been
all the more eager to make an example of me, to discourage any such insubordinate notions among the other
junior officers."

"Well, your military career is over, just the same."

"That was my own free choice. I gave them more than
six years of faithful duty in exchange for my four-year
education at the Point, so I guess we're all about even."
He finished his stewed apples, wiped his mouth on his
napkin, and pushed his plate aside with a sigh. "That was
delicious." He leaned back in his chair and looked across
the table at Cathy. "So now I'm putting all that behind
me and I'm ready for a fresh start."

"At what?" Cathy asked, catching his eyes.

"I'm not real sure. But after spending all that time in

the Third Cavalry trying to defend these crazy civilian prospectors from the Indians, I may try a little prospecting myself." He grinnned, showing his white, even teeth. "I feel like a kid who's just been let out of school for summer vacation. What about you, Wiley?"

"No plans. But as long as we're this close to all this gold, I'm all for giving it a try. No sense letting somebody else have it all." He blew a thin stream of blue smoke at the ceiling. "Picking up gold sure beats mule packing for a living."

"I was hoping you'd say that. I've never had friends like the three of you in all my adult life," Curt said. He stopped, as though he couldn't trust himself to go on. I was somewhat surprised. I had come to know him as a steady, reliable friend, but he seldom showed emotion. Maybe he was finally beginning to show his true personality, cracking the shell he had formed around himself as a company commander.

"Then it's settled," Curt continued, looking around at us eagerly. "We'll throw in together, buy some gear, and try our luck on some of the creeks around here."

"Done!" I held out my hand, and the four of us gripped hands together.

"How about a drink to seal the bargain?" Wiley suggested. "I need something to cut the trail dust out of my throat."

"Dust? You haven't seen any dust in at least six weeks."

"Well, mud then."

We paid for our meal with more of our greenbacks and then stepped across the street to the Golden Eagle Saloon. It was a deep, narrow, high-ceilinged room, with the heavy, dark wooden bar running most of the way along one wall. There was no foot rail, but three brass spittoons were set at convenient spots. As my eyes adjusted to the dimmer light and began to take in more details, I saw the bartender break off his conversation with one of his customers and come toward us. "What'll it be?"

"I don't suppose you have any cognac, do you?" Wiley asked without a trace of a smile.

"Not at the moment," the bartender answered, also deadpan, so I couldn't tell if he thought Wiley was joking or serious. For all I knew, he might have just run out of cognac.

"Whiskey, then."

The bartender pointed at the rest of us and arched his eyebrows.

We ordered beer. We leaned on the bar and watched the bartender work. He was a barrel-chested man with massive arms and shoulders, but he moved with the grace and economy of motion of a man who is completely at home in the small space behind a bar. He wore a full, dark beard tinged with gray on the sides, and a drooping walrus mustache. His hair, thinning on top, was worn somewhat long on the sides, curling around his ears and just brushing his collar in back.

The white shirt he wore was set off by a maroon vest and matching maroon sleeve garters. The shirt was open at the collar, but the short neck was hidden behind the beard. His sleeves were rolled up on the forearms, revealing thick, curly black hair. The whole impression I formed in a matter of seconds was of a genial bear of a man with great physical strength.

"There ya are, gents," he said, sliding the foamy mugs across the polished wood toward us. He had already poured Wiley his whiskey. He glanced at Cathy and then back at us. "I don't want no trouble in here, now."

"Whatdya mean?" Wiley demanded, instantly on the defensive.

"No offense," he replied, holding up his hand, "but we don't serve many ladies in here. And a lot of these men haven't seen a good-looking woman for quite a spell. You know what I mean."

"Don't worry. She's with us. And we won't be staying long," Curt said.

"We'll stay as long as we damn well please," Wiley said belligerently, tossing off his drink and pouring himself another from the bottle on the bar before Cathy pulled him toward a table.

"Be quiet!" she scolded. "Anyone would think you're drunk already. He was just giving us a friendly warning. And I, for one, am glad he did." She looked around at the other men in the place. There were only about three tables occupied—maybe eight or nine men, some of them playing cards and some just drinking and talking. Several of them had looked up at Wiley's outburst, but had now resumed their own pursuits. One or two stared boldly at Cathy, then said something to each other and they all laughed.

We sat and drank our beer down quickly before lingering over a refill. Wiley had the bartender bring the bottle to the table.

"We'll need some picks and shovels and pans, and some tools to build some kind of a shelter," Curt was saying. "Even with the prices as they are around here, we should be able to afford the basic necessities for long enough to see if we're going to show enough color to stake a claim."

"I imagine most of the creeks in this area that are any good are already staked out," I said.

We discussed the items we would need and tried to figure in our heads the approximate cost. We plotted and planned and dreamed of the coming days and weeks. The longer we talked, the more gold fever seemed to grip us, even though the only gold we had seen was the small number of fine grains we had received as change.

The pendulum clock on a shelf behind the bar was pointing at 4:40 when I suddenly became aware of a commotion outside. People were yelling and shouting, and I heard what sounded like cheering and whistling. Horses galloped past the door. The sound of running feet thundered hollowly on the board walks.

The bat-wing doors flew inward and a man burst in.

"C'mon, Burnie, they're here. They're coming up the gulch!"

The bartender started around the end of the bar, and then stopped, as if remembering the unguarded cash drawer.

"Who's coming?" he hollered.

The man had jumped back outside and was looking down the street. Then he stuck his head back inside.

"Dammit, Burnett, come on if you want to see General Buck! By God, the whole damn cavalry is acomin' up Main Street right now!"

CHAPTER 4

I jumped to my feet, nearly upsetting our table, as the other men in the room rushed past us toward the door.

"Come on, Curt, let's get out of here!" I urged.

Wiley and Cathy were getting to their feet, startled looks on their faces.

But Curt hardly moved. He acted almost as if he hadn't heard. He sipped his beer and continued to stare straight ahead.

"What's wrong? Let's go."

He finally looked up. Then, without hurrying, he drained his mug and stood up. "Okay, I'm ready. But I just hate to hide like a hunted animal. It really galls me. I've never had to tuck my tail and run in my life. I just hate to start now."

I could see he was getting his back up and might do something stupidly defiant, so I tried another tack. "Look, we're just using common sense. We'll just step over to the room and stay out of sight for a while. We don't want any trouble with them. It'll ruin all our plans."

He didn't answer, but I could see the set of his jaw as we walked toward the door and pushed our way outside.

It seemed the whole town was rushing toward the lower end of the gulch. The yelling and cheering continued, while some exuberant riders wheeled their horses in a circle, firing their guns into the air.

But the blue-coated saviors they were welcoming were a sorry-looking bunch of heroes. The bedraggled column that approached was in even worse shape than when we had left it. The men were thin, ragged, and bearded.

36

Most of them were walking, leading what few horses they still had. And the horses were shuffling along, their heads hanging, looking as if they could barely put one foot ahead of another. As they came closer, I could pick out three or four individuals I recognized, before the crowd of townspeople surrounded them.

We were still standing in the doorway on the shaded boardwalk, and bartender Burnett had come to the door and was looking out, talking to another man near us.

"Dawson and some of the boys rode out to meet 'em with a couple wagonloads of food and a few cattle yesterday afternoon," the man was saying. "They been havin' a pretty tough time of it."

"Yeah. They look it," Burnett agreed.

"I hear they been fightin' Crazy Horse all summer. By durn, we won't have to worry about them Injuns while they're here, at least. I feel a lot safer already. By durn, nothin's too good for those boys!"

I was getting nervous, and pulled Curt's arm, but he hung back, staring down the street as if fascinated by the sight of his former outfit. Then I saw what he was looking at. General Buck was mounted on his black charger and was still visible above the heads of the crowd. And close beside him was Curt's old nemesis, Major Zimmer.

"You might know he'd be riding," I said to Curt. "He sure as hell isn't going to walk as long as there's one horse left standing."

The troops and the surging crowd overflowed the entire street and the sidewalks. We were rather well covered by the bodies milling around us. The whole mob crawled to a stop in front of the Grand Central Hotel about three doors down and across from us. General Buck dismounted and shook hands with a tall man in a black coat and hat whom I took to be some local dignitary, possibly the mayor. Major Zimmer and a few of the other officers and men remained mounted. The rest of the companies continued to stream in from the north end of town in ragged groups of twos and threes.

We were probably no more than thirty or forty yards from the front of the Grand Central. Zimmer had his hat on, throwing his face in deeper shade, even though the late afternoon sun had already dropped behind the western ridge, throwing the whole street into shadow. In a minute or so Zimmer's horse sidled around until he was facing our direction, and Zimmer appeared to be looking right at us. I felt a tingle up my spine until I realized that he couldn't see us as we stood far back under the shelter of the boardwalk. Then he took off his hat and wiped a sleeve across his forehead. Apparently, Wilder was having mixed feelings, because he half turned toward me and said, "You know, there are a lot of my old friends and comrades-in-arms over there, but I feel a curious detachment from them, as if I had been away from them for years, instead of just three days or so."

I thought his face bore a sad look, lonesome for a time that would never come again. Curt continued watching for a few more seconds, and then seemed to shake himself out of his reverie and become his old, practical self again. "From the looks of their mounts, they're going to be buying up every available horse in town. If we want something to ride, we'd better get down to the livery stable—fast."

"What about that Indian pony herd they captured at Slim Buttes?" Wiley asked as the four of us headed toward the opposite end of town and the stable.

"They'll probably use them until they can get a replacement supply of full-sized horses from the Department of the Platte. I'm sure General Buck'll send a wire for some before the day is out."

We found the livery stable operator in the process of locking up his business so he could join the general celebration, and he was a little irritated when we showed up.

"We want to sell you that Indian pony we left and buy two horses," Curt said. "And we need saddles too, if you've got 'em."

He hesitated, looking down the street. "Well . . . okay, come on in." He swung the big door open and we went inside. "Haven't got many," the stable operator said.

"Only need two," Curt replied.

"Two?" Wiley asked.

"We can get by with two," Curt answered, speaking aside to us, quietly. "We need to watch our expenses so we won't have to work while we do some prospecting."

"Here's a fine-looking animal here," the owner was saying, leading out a sorrel Morgan from a stall.

Wiley and Curt went over him carefully, feeling his legs and looking at his teeth. I was a complete novice at horse-trading, but he looked like a fine animal to me—well fleshed and not swaybacked.

"Well?" I asked when they had completed their inspection.

"How much?" Curt asked, without replying to my question.

"A hundred dollars," came the prompt answer.

"Including saddle and bridle?"

"No. That'd be a hundred and thirty-five."

"Highway robbery."

"No, it's not. A good used saddle and bridle is worth every bit of thirty-five."

"I mean the horse."

"But that's as fine an animal as you'll find in the Hills!"

"What's wrong with him?"

"Nothing."

Curt said nothing—just eyed the animal again, and then walked slowly over to him and ran his hand down along the length of his back. The horse swished his tail and shivered a muscle at a fly, but otherwise didn't move. Curt walked around behind him and came back and stood in front of the Morgan with his hands on his hips. Then he drew my .44 Colt from his belt, aimed it at the ceiling, and fired two quick shots. The explosions were deafening in the closed space.

All the horses in the stalls jerked their heads up, but the Morgan went absolutely wild. He reared on his hind feet, lunged, and made for the nearest door. Finding his way blocked, he brought his hooves crashing down against the wood, knocking splinters from it. Then he came down on all fours and aimed a vicious kick out behind him and raced toward the other end of the stable. He reared and let out a whinny that was almost a squeal, then came tearing back toward us. We all scattered and ran for the walls and climbed the sides of the stalls.

"What the hell'd you do that for?" the owner was screaming over the commotion.

The horse ran back and forth two or three more times, but finding escape impossible, he finally stopped at the far end of the barn and stood quivering and looking wild-eyed at us, his ears pricked forward.

Curt climbed down from his spot on the loft ladder and slipped some bills from his billfold.

"Here's a hundred. Take it or leave it."

The fat owner hesitated, but when Curt started to put the money away, he reached for it quickly and turned away, muttering under his breath.

"Throw a saddle and bridle on him when he calms down, and in the meantime I'll be looking over your stock of mules."

"Have you got a bill of sale for that pony you want to trade?"

"No," Curt replied. "He's an Indian pony we found running wild on the plains northeast of here."

"How can I be sure of that?"

"If you'll take a good look at him, you can tell he's never been owned by a white man."

Wiley, who was more of an authority on mules, picked out a good one, and after more haggling, Curt paid the owner another seventy dollars difference for him and a double-rigged McClellan saddle.

When we had signed the appropriate papers and were leading our two animals from the barn, I could contain my curiosity no longer.

"How did you know there was something wrong with that horse, Curt?"

"Did you notice that brand on his hip?"

"Yeah. It says 'U.S.' He's an old cavalry horse."

"I mean the other brand just below it."

I looked again. "Oh, yes. I didn't know what it was. Looks like the letters I. C."

"That's right. It stands for Inspected and Condemned. The Quartermaster Corps has found him unfit for army service. But at first I couldn't figure out why. He's not over four years old, and he appeared to be sound in limb and wind. And then it finally came to me. A lot of horses are rejected because they can never get used to the sound of gunfire. And that's a fatal flaw for a cavalry horse. I guessed right about this one."

"Where are we going to keep these animals?" Wiley asked. "Don't you want to leave them at the livery?"

"No. He'll probably jack up the price of boarding them because I got 'em for a little less money. Besides, you never know what the night will bring. I want them handy in case we need them in a hurry for some reason," Curt replied.

Wiley and Cathy and I looked our questions at each other. What could possibly happen? It was okay to be prepared, but I thought Curt was getting a little overly cautious.

There was a somewhat level, grassy area behind our hotel at the base of the steeper hill. It was here that Curt and Wiley picketed the horse and mule for the night before we retired to our rooms. All of us gathered in Cathy's corner room and moved our chairs near the window to have a good view of Main Street. As night gradually came on, we could see more people arriving from the north end of town, apparently from the creeks and Crook City. The people were getting ready to really give a welcoming celebration to the long-awaited troops. Bonfires flared up on the hillsides and even in the street. I could hear the steam whistle from the sawmill sounding off. Soldiers surged up and down the street in groups and mingled with the citizens. Every few minutes the concussion of an explosion blasted our ears as someone set off a powder charge on an anvil.

The last light of day, combining with the wavering light of the bonfires below us, showed that there were more women in Deadwood than I had originally thought. Both the upper and lower windows of the saloons, eating houses, wash houses, and the Grand Central Hotel were crowded with them—women of all ages and appearances. I noticed Cathy eyeing these women also.

"What do you think?" I asked.

"About what?"

"Those women. Are they wives, mothers, cooks, laundresses, ladies of the evening? What are they all doing in a town two hundred and fifty miles from the nearest railroad in an area surrounded by hostile Indians?"

"I hate to say it, but I imagine that most of them are harlots. I've seen the type in other frontier mining camps —the ones who are too old or ugly to practice their trade in more civilized towns." She gave a little shudder. "I feel so sorry for them. They're really pitiful."

"Well, there may be some of them here on legitimate business," I said to brighten her up. "I saw two women dealing blackjack in a couple of the places we passed today. And there were some women cooks at the Grand Central, where we ate, too."

"You can't really believe those hard-looking harpies are actually honest working women?" She was incredulous. "The cooks may be, and there are probably some storekeepers' wives here, though," she conceded. "And now and then I suppose a woman could wind up in a place like this due to some odd set of circumstances. Look at me. Four months ago I never would have dreamed I would be here, especially with the likes of you." She laughed and gave me a shove.

We were interrupted by a chant set up by the crowd in the street below us: "We want Buck! We want Buck! We want Buck!"

The chant was taken up by others, until the whole street rocked with the voices of some two thousand people shouting in unison.

And they didn't have long to wait. In two or three minutes the chant broke into wild cheering as the bearded general appeared on the balcony of the Grand Central Hotel. He began to address the crowd, but we were too far away to catch more than a word or two now and then. He was interrupted often by laughter and applause.

Shortly after he finished speaking, General Buck and

several of the officers who were staying at the Grand Central were escorted by some of the town officials to some waiting buggies and driven off toward the upper end of town where they disappeared from our sight.

"Probably going to take in a show at that big tent theater just beyond the cemetery," Curt surmised. "Except for the hell holes on Main Street, it's probably the only entertainment in town."

"Where are the rest of the troops staying?" Wiley asked. "The officers probably got all the hotel space."

"They're camped just out of town on one of the creeks, I'd guess. At least, those that haven't got the strength or inclination to spend the night in town drinking and gambling and blowing their summer's pay."

I backed away from the window and struck a match to the coal-oil lamp, and the darkening room sprang into light again. Then I tore a piece off my old shirttail and proceeded to clean my rifle. Curt joined me in cleaning my Colt. We got them pretty thoroughly dried out to prevent any rusting, but lacked anything we could use in the way of a cleaning rod for the rifle. And we had no oil. But we compromised by pouring a little coal oil from the lamp down the barrel and on all the moving parts to give them a protective coating until we could get something better.

"I hope the troops move out of here tomorrow. I don't want to stay cooped up in this room for a couple of days or longer."

"You and me both."

There was too much noise in our hotel and up and down the street for any real sleep that night, but we decided to give it a try, anyway. As a precaution, Wiley slept with my rifle on the floor in his sister's room, and Curt and I shared the other room and kept the revolver.

In spite of the occasional gunshots that brought me up, tense, and the drunken shouting and banging around in the hallways and other rooms of our hotel, I finally slept sometime after midnight. The last thing I remember was the faint sound of several voices trying to sing to the accompaniment of a hurdy-gurdy.

CHAPTER 5

I awoke to silence and opened my eyes to full daylight and a cool breeze rustling the curtains at the window. I had slept so soundly that it took me a minute or two to remember where I was, as I rolled over on the floor and threw back the quilt I had wrapped myself in. I stretched, got up, and went to the window in my long johns. The breeze carried the fresh smell of pine. Even though the Hills were known for their rain and snow, the weather had relented for the time being and the blue sky contained only a few small fluffy clouds. From the angle of the sun on the buildings across the street, I guessed it was at least nine o'clock. I had been more tired than I realized.

I glanced around at Curt, but he was still dead to the world. When I looked back at the street, I was suddenly struck by the absence of people, especially for this time of morning. I saw two or three pedestrians, and as I looked, a lone horseman passed down the street. Apparently, the whole town was sleeping off its celebration of the night before. Or they were all at work somewhere.

It wasn't until a half-hour later, when the four of us had dressed and gone down the street to breakfast, that we discovered the soldiers had departed early that morning. They were on the way south toward Custer City, much to my relief and the relief of Curt and the two Jenkinses.

After breakfast we retrieved our horse and mule from behind the hotel and went shopping for provisions. We bought rice and sugar and coffee, onions, dried beans and canned tomatoes, shovels and picks, a compass,

matches, bedrolls, ponchos, tin mess-gear and pans, bacon
and flour, and, optimistically, another small buckskin
pouch for gold. We also replenished our ammunition
and bought another good, used Colt .44 and two holsters
and belts. I made a leather loop for my Winchester on
the Morgan's saddle.

Wiley, with much experience as a mule packer, rigged
a homemade wooden pack saddle, removed the light
McClellan, and lashed the pack expertly on our mule. The
whole load didn't weigh much over 120 pounds.

While Wiley was rigging our pack, the rest of us made
some discreet inquiries of the hotel clerk about gold
prospects in the area. But he had come to Deadwood only
two weeks before, and knew next to nothing about it. He
was a small, thin man, who appeared more interested in
making his money from behind a counter than on the
business end of a shovel.

"How about the claims office?" Cathy suggested as we
stood in the middle of the street, undecided about which
way to start out. "At least they'll know which claims have
already been staked." It struck me as the most practical
suggestion we had heard.

But this proved to be less than enlightening. Since we
weren't familiar with the names or locations of most of
the creeks, or the details of the topography, the information we got did not help us that much.

"Let's drop in at the Golden Eagle Saloon and ask
Burnett," Wiley suggested.

"Who's Burnett?"

"Pat Burnett—you know—the bartender. Bartenders
know everything."

"Good idea."

"Is Jenkins an Irish name?" Curt asked Wiley as we
tied our mounts to a hitching rail out front.

"English. Why?"

"You can think of some of the darndest reasons to get
a drink."

"It *is* hot out here," he said with a grin.

The Golden Eagle was dark and cool, and Burnett was
sitting on a stool behind the bar with nothing to do.

"Business a little slow?"

"So far. But we had enough last night to last about three days," he answered, stifling a yawn. "Coulda used a little more sleep this morning myself."

We ordered a beer and began to pump him about prospecting sites. As it turned out, he had been in Deadwood since its founding and was familiar with most of the region.

"I do a good bit of prospecting myself whenever I get a chance," he told us. " 'Course I'm not going to tell you where my favorite spot is, 'cause I'm getting ready to stake a claim myself if it pans out. But if I was you, I'd head south of town, a little deeper into the hills. The creeks up north toward Crook City are pretty well staked out, but there's some likely-looking country a little farther south. There are prospectors in there now, but they are the brave or foolish ones. Until the troops came, the Indians was killin' off most of the men who went out there. As a matter of fact, and near as anybody can estimate, we've had about four hundred people killed by Indians in the Hills just this year. Folks coming into town nearly every day reportin' scalped bodies in the remote canyons or along the trails."

We looked at each other significantly.

"You wouldn't be joshin' us a little, now would you?" Wiley asked, "just to scare us off your prospectin' territory?"

"Nope," he replied soberly. He waved his hand in a general southerly direction. "There's plenty gold out there for anyone who has the guts to go look for it. I'd probably be out there every day if I wasn't so fond of keeping what hair I have left. The Sioux and Cheyenne are really sore about us taking their hills. In fact, the first preacher in town, Reverend Smith, was killed and scalped last month. He was just walkin' up the gulch one afternoon to preach at the next town, but he never got there. A miner found his body along the road next day and brought him in."

He went on to tell us the general lay of the land. He even got out a pencil and paper and sketched from memory the major creeks and canyons, indicating the corduroy road that snaked a sinuous way south to Custer City, some sixty miles away.

Curt thanked him, folded the map, and was tucking it away when the bat-wing doors flew open and four men burst in, talking and laughing loudly. Ignoring us, they shoved up to the bar and ordered whiskey. They were dirty and unshaven and obviously had been drinking for some time. Burnett went to wait on them, and they paid for their drinks with greenbacks. I took a closer look at them. Under the dirt and grime, they were wearing remnants of cavalry uniforms. Apparently they were deserters, or else had been lying drunk somewhere in town when the regiment moved out this morning.

As the man closest to us threw back his head and gulped the jigger down, his bloodshot eyes fastened on Cathy.

"Hey, gal, kin I buy ya a drink?" he leered, showing tobacco-stained teeth.

"No." She moved away from his hand, which was reaching for her arm.

"Aw, c'mon, baby, let's you and me have some fun. I got money." His companions looked on, grinning.

I noticed they were still wearing their standard-issue Colts. "Better leave her alone," I cautioned him as I noticed the look in Curt's and Wiley's eyes. "She doesn't work in here. She's with us."

For the first time, he looked at me. "Get your own girl," he said, shortly. "I just asked this girl to have a drink with me." He glared at me, his hand dropping toward his gun belt.

"Back off, Private Arnold!"

The voice at my shoulder cracked like a whip.

The man's jaw dropped slightly and his eyes shifted to Curt's face. As recognition slowly penetrated the alcoholic haze, his slack-jawed surprise at being called by name slowly changed to an arrogant grin.

"Well, by God! Boys, look who it is. Old Cap'n Wilder himself. Fancy meetin' you here. Have a drink with us— now that we're all in the same boat, so to speak." He winked familiarly and laughed. His three companions had still not spoken.

"Get out of my sight!" Curt said in a low, deadly tone.

Arnold turned his head toward his friends, and in mock seriousness said, "Can you imagine an Injun-lovin' deserter bein' too good to drink with us?"

Wilder's jaw muscles tightened and I eased back out of the way. But Arnold's friends, who were not as drunk as he, saw the dangerous turn things were taking.

"Come on, Milo, we don't want any trouble. Let's get out of here," one urged.

"Yeh. I met a couple o' girls down at Myra's place last night. Let's go down there," another one said, taking him by the arm.

But Arnold shook off the hand. "Not until I teach this uppity sonuvabitch a lesson," he snarled.

Curt and I were the only ones of our group who were armed. Wiley pulled Cathy off to one side, away from the bar. From a glance at his face, I knew he wanted to get into the fight, but he also knew this would not be settled with fists. Arnold's friends also had moved aside.

"You're drunk. Get out of here," Curt said as if dismissing the whole thing.

"Not till I teach you a lesson, you smart-mouthed, Injun-lovin' West Pointer. You're no damn better than we are. You deserted just like the rest of us. Only difference is, we didn't leave 'cause we were afraid to fight. We'd just had enough of you and all your officer buddies treatin' us like niggers."

I could see Curt's face growing slightly redder, and I knew the man was getting to him. But none of the rest of us said anything. As long as it was between the two of them, it was a fair fight. Even Burnett, who, I'm sure, had a shotgun behind the bar, was not interfering.

Finally, Curt turned away from the bar and faced his tormentor. "Okay, *private*, you've had your say. Now make your move or crawl out of here with your tail between your legs!"

With a choking cry of rage, Arnold reached for his gun. Curt leaped to his right as he grabbed for his own

Colt. Arnold's gun roared a split second ahead of Curt's,
but Arnold was the one who staggered back, clutching at
his right thigh with his free hand. Curt's gun roared
again as Arnold raised his gun for a second shot. Arnold
fired. Both men missed, and through the cloud of powder
smoke I saw the front window disappear in a shower of
glass. When his leg gave way, Arnold had caught himself
from falling by hooking his right elbow on the bar. As
he braced his arm along the bar and cocked his gun to
fire again, Wilder leaped forward and brought his gun
barrel down on the soldier's right wrist, knocking the
revolver loose. It skidded across the polished wood and
fell behind the bar. Then Curt brought his gun barrel up,
pistol-whipping him across the right temple, knocking him
to the floor, where he lay half-stunned.

The fight was over, and Curt stood, breathing heavily,
as Arnold's friends rushed to his aid. I saw Burnett relax
his grip on something below the bar, and I looked at
Wiley and Cathy, who were just getting up from behind
an overturned table. I had been so interested in the fight,
I had forgotten to take cover during the few seconds it
lasted.

My ears were still ringing from the explosions and my
nose stinging from the acrid powder when I heard a
thundering of hooves outside and looked up to see a six-
horse hitch gallop by at full speed, pulling a stagecoach.
In a second, the fight was forgotten, and I ran for the
door. I didn't know what was wrong, but I had never seen
a coach driven full tilt through a town that way.

As I hit the bright sunlight in the street, other men
were running from buildings, looking toward the runaway.
I caught a glimpse of someone's back on the box, someone
apparently trying to halt the flying team. Two men on
horseback finally caught up with the lead horses as the
coach neared the lower end of Main Street. Before the
team could be stopped, the stage had careened out of
sight around a bend in the street.

Wiley, Cathy, and Curt joined me a couple of minutes
later as the riders were leading the team and the coach
back up toward us and the Wells Fargo stage station.

I glanced back at the door of the Golden Eagle Saloon and saw Burnett directing the four soldiers up the street, evidently toward the doctor's office, as three of them half carried the wounded, white-faced Arnold up the boardwalk. A bloody blue bandanna had been tied around his thigh inside the slit pants leg.

As the coach was led past us, we saw a hatless, black-suited man sitting on the box holding the reins. From the way he looked and the way he handled the lines, I knew he was no driver. His face was drawn and white with fear, and his gray hair blew around in his eyes in the swirling wind.

The four of us automatically followed the coach, and others joined the parade until, when the red Concord was brought to a halt in front of the stage station, the lathered horses stamping and tossing their heads, a sizable crowd had collected.

Everyone was yelling at once, about half of them asking what happened and the other half shouting for them to shut up and let the driver talk. In the midst of all this confusion someone climbed up and set the brake, took the reins from the black-suited man, and hooked them around the brake handle. Others helped the man down. He looked as if he were going to collapse. Then we saw why the driver looked so shaken. The bodies of the regular driver and the shotgun messenger were lying under his feet in the boot. Several willing hands lifted the two dead men down and laid them out on the boardwalk. One of them had a neat hole in the center of his forehead, and the other's vest and shirt were a mass of blood. I looked away, feeling a little queasy.

A man with a sheriff's badge and someone I took to be the express agent were questioning the black-suited man. As we crowded in closer, I could hear snatches of the conversation.

". . . hit us while we were changing horses at Ten-Mile Station. Yeah, yeah—Fitzgerald's place. No, no warning. They must've been inside the station."

"What about the gold?" someone yelled. A buzz went

through the crowd, as if this information were not general knowledge.

"They got the strongbox, if that's what was in it," the black-suited man said.

"God! A month's worth of dust—gone!"

"Is Wells Fargo going to reimburse me for this?" someone else yelled.

"Let's get up a posse!" a man near me shouted.

A chorus of seconds greeted this proposal.

The four of us had seen enough and slipped back out of the crowd.

"This isn't our problem," Curt said. "Let's go. We need to locate a good campsite before dark."

Cathy mounted the horse; her brother led the pack mule while Curt and I walked. After we were several hundred yards away, I looked back at the excited crowd that still surrounded the coach. It struck me that the clump of buzzing humanity looked strangely small and insignificant in proportion to the surrounding hills rising above the buildings. From this perspective, their fighting over the shiny yellow metal shrank to the grossest absurdity.

But we were all going out looking for this same metal, I thought as we turned a bend in the street and the crowd was lost to sight.

We followed the road out of town and tramped along for an hour or so as the easy grade wound along the bottom of the canyon. We spoke very little. I think everyone was thinking over the events of the day and the past few days, wondering what lay ahead.

"What's wrong, Curt? You look worried," I said as we walked a few yards ahead of the Jenkinses.

He looked up blankly. Then his face became animated, as if he were coming back from a long way off. "Worried? Oh, no, no. I was just thinking about that gunfight." He paused.

"Yeah?"

"I'm just a little shaky, I guess," he said quietly, almost as if he were ashamed of the feeling.

"Well, it was a pure case of self-defense," I reminded

him, aware of his strong aversion to killing. This aversion had caused him to end his army career only the week before.

"I know, I know. That's not what bothers me."

"Then what? You only wounded him. And it didn't even look too serious."

"That's it. I wasn't trying to wound him. I was just trying to hit him—anywhere. It never entered my mind at the time to try to wound him."

"Don't worry about it. Everybody has the instinct for survival. And you're no professional gunfighter, so you haven't had much practice with a handgun at close range —especially with somebody shooting back."

He pondered that for a few seconds.

"Guess you're right," he finally conceded. "I was probably lucky to hit anything, because I remember jumping to one side just as we both drew."

"I know one thing."

"What's that?"

"He was sure aimin' to drill you dead center."

"He was either a mighty bad shot, or just too drunk— or both."

I grinned. "As drunk as he looked, he may not have even hit the back wall. I was probably in more danger than you were."

Curt's face relaxed into a grin. "You're probably right. By the way, since it was my bullet that knocked out Burnett's front window, I left him ten dollars to help pay for it. Told him if it came to more than that, I'd reimburse him later."

"Does he own the place?"

"Yeah. Said he'd have to order the glass, so he'd just board it up in the meantime."

"Reckon we shoulda reported that shooting to the sheriff?" I asked.

"Naw. Nobody was killed. And besides, he's got more important things on his mind now. From what I gathered, the population of that town is reduced by one or two every night anyway, and as long as it's not out-and-out murder, nobody else gets too excited about it. The law isn't too strong here, and apparently the vigilantes haven't gotten organized yet."

Even as we walked along at a relaxed pace and talked, I noticed Curt's eyes constantly sweeping the wooded hills on either side of the road. Then I recalled what Burnett had told us about the Sioux' killing so many prospectors in the area, and the dark green, scented trees around us suddenly became the ominous hiding places of hostile eyes. I almost felt a chill in the hot, sparkling sunshine of the September day.

After consulting the crude map Burnett had drawn for us, we decided to strike off the road toward the west. We blundered into a couple of blind canyons and had to back up and detour. It was rugged going for about two hours, up and down steep, rocky ridges. I was glad we were off the road and traveling cross-country: whether it was true or not, the cover of trees and boulders gave me a feeling of security from ambush by hostiles or robbers.

I guessed it was about four o'clock when we slid down a steep, shale-covered hillside and descended into a shallow, grassy valley. A mountain stream flowed down from a cleft in the granite ridge at the southwest end of the valley and ran, splashing and gurgling, down its center until its flow was quieted by the level valley floor. Fir and pine rimmed the valley and grew about a third of the way down the slopes before they thinned out and the grass took over.

Almost as one, we stopped and stared at the beautiful pastoral scene before us.

"Looks like a good place to start."

The feeling was unanimous.

"Even if there's no gold here, it'd be a beautiful place to camp," Cathy remarked as we started toward the far end of the valley where the stream cascaded down out of the trees. The valley was narrow—only about four hundred yards across—actually a grassy canyon. Nor were we the first to discover this Eden. There was a thin column of smoke from a campfire and the tiny figures of two men moving in and out of the trees along the stream.

As we led our animals along the bank of the stream, the figures disappeared into the trees, and I got the same skin-crawling feeling that had come over me when we were approaching the hidden war party of Sioux along the Belle Fourche. The feeling of unseen muzzles trained on me was something I could never get used to.

When we approached close enough to be seen clearly, two men stepped out from behind some big pines with rifles leveled at us. We stopped.

"What're y'all up to?" a tall, lean, hard-eyed man demanded. His shirt was dirty and too short in the sleeves, revealing big bony wrists.

"Just doing a little prospecting, like yourselves," Curt answered, casually indicating the rocker in the edge of the stream.

"Just come out from Deadwood?" the man asked, still eyeing us suspiciously. He lowered his Winchester slightly. His shorter companion, who wore a black felt hat with the brim bent down all around, kept his rifle steady.

"Yeah," Curt answered.

"We got a claim staked here," the big man continued, still unsmiling, but not sounding hostile now. "There's our lower marker. You're welcome to prospect anywhere below that."

He turned away abruptly, and his partner with the hat followed without a word. They leaned their Winchesters against a tree within reach and returned quickly to work, almost as if we had wasted some of their precious, gold-seeking daylight. And I could understand their feeling; in spite of the sun, there was a smell of fall in the air.

We unpacked our mule and set up camp on the grassy slope about seventy yards below, where the curve of the slope began to gentle out.

"Hope they haven't got all the gold," Wiley said, digging into the pack for a pan. "They may have worked this section before they staked their claim."

"I doubt if they got it all. Besides, there are creeks all through these hills."

"Yeh. But how many of 'em are gold-bearing?"

"That's what we're here to find out. Gold is where you

find it. Nobody at first thought there was any color as far north in the Hills as Deadwood Gulch. Now look at it."

Cathy and I carried some small rocks from the timber-line and the creek to make a fire-ring, while Curt and Wiley got right down to business and began panning up and down the stream. When we had our gear pretty well arranged and a fire laid, Cathy and I joined in and we all hunkered down, swirling the sand and gravel of the stream bed, straining our eyes for the telltale glitter, or for the slight trace of yellow residue of black dirt and sand. But we found nothing.

"Oh, man, this is killin' my back!" Wiley groaned, straightening up and shaking out his pan. It was growing too dark to see, and we hadn't found the slightest trace.

"We know there's gold washed down from that ridge, or those two above us wouldn't have bothered to stake a claim."

"You're right."

We all pitched in with renewed energy, but darkness shortly forced us to quit. We cooked supper and rolled into our bedrolls, exhausted from the day's toil.

It was late the next afternoon before we struck our first color.

CHAPTER 6

It was Curt who first found it. Instead of the trace of dust we were expecting, the elusive gold appeared in the gravel of his pan in the form of a small nugget about the size of the tip of his little finger. It had tiny veins of white quartz running through it, but had been scoured smooth and nearly round by the action of the stream.

This renewed our enthusiasm, but our next three hours of constant labor were rewarded with only the slightest traces of dust, worth no more than a dollar or two, we estimated, based on the current twenty-dollars-per-ounce price.

"The way I figure it, the heavy metal dropped to bedrock higher up; the water wasn't flowing swift enough to carry it down here," Wiley said as we were preparing for supper.

"You forget that we're talking about thousands, or probably millions, of years. No telling what kind of changes, upheavals, and erosions have taken place. This hill didn't always slope just the way it does now," Curt said. "That's the fun of prospecting: Nobody—not even the mineral experts and geologists—know where it is. They can only speculate, based on what types of formations it's been found in before."

"Well, if you ask me," Wiley answered, "gold prospecting is like fishing: It's only fun if you're having some luck."

The next morning we were up and at it early, and stayed at it until dark without pausing for anything but a drink of water now and then. But the day's labor again proved almost fruitless. Our day's take of dust amounted to no more than two or three dollars. We estimated our total take, counting the small nugget, at about fifteen dollars.

Our aching backs told us that at this rate we would never make it in this prospecting business.

"But that's just it," Wiley argued as we sat around our campfire that night. "Prospecting isn't a business. It's a gamble. Maybe that's why I like it so much already, in spite of the way my back feels." He shifted into a more comfortable position against the saddle he was leaning on. "If I were working for wages, I wouldn't put in one more minute at this. But, just think"—he leaned forward to emphasize his point—"the next panful of gravel may be a ten-dollar or a twenty-dollar one. We know the gold is here and there all around us in these hills. All we have to do is find it."

"Oh, is that all? How simple!" Cathy said sarcastically.

"Yeah."

"I don't know how you got so optimistic all of a sudden," she rejoined.

"Well, 'Blessed is he who expects nothing, for he shall never be disappointed,' " Curt quoted.

"Where did you hear that?" Wiley asked.

"Ben Franklin's *Poor Richard's Almanac*," he replied. "And don't look so surprised. They teach other things besides engineering at West Point. And I've done a little reading in my time, too."

"Well, I expect *something* and I'm not planning on being disappointed," Wiley said with finality.

"I tell you what," Curt suggested, "why don't we scout around tomorrow and see what other streams may be in this area. It can't hurt. We can always come back here if we want to."

After some discussion, this was agreed on and we turned in.

The next day Wiley and I took the horse and mule and set off westward, leaving Curt and Cathy, with most of the arms, to continue working the stream.

We must have ridden seven or eight miles vertically, but only about three or four horizontally, that day. About midafternoon, we came upon another little valley, about half the size of the one we had left. And this one, too, had a promising little stream that was doing its patient work of carving the little valley deeper.

It took us only a few minutes to unlimber our gear and start panning. I struck a little color in the very first panful. Wiley had started about fifteen yards upstream from me.

"Yeow! We've hit it! Matt, look!" He threw his hat on the ground and splashed out of the edge of the water, holding the pan out for me to see. I ran up as he set the pan down and began clawing out the larger rocks and debris. "Here, let me wash it down a little finer and you can see."

He stooped and scooped up a little water and carefully swished it around in the shallow pan, letting a little more of the sand and water flip over the rim with each swirl. I watched eagerly over his shoulder, my heart pounding with excitement. As the lighter dirt and sand was sluiced off, the finely ground yellow metal spread itself in a glittering fan across the dark bottom. We both caught our breath at the sight.

We carefully sifted the dust into our rawhide poke, and tried several more panfuls at different points along the creek. In less than an hour we had collected at least an ounce. Our pans varied from point to point and sometime came up empty, but this hardly dampened our enthusiasm.

"This has gotta be a fifty-dollar diggins," Wiley said.

Since it was already late afternoon, we continued panning until dark and then made camp for the night, being careful to build our small fire up close to one steep hillside of the narrow canyon. We scraped away the dry pine needles and made a rock fire-ring before making our fire under a huge pine where it would be least visible.

Whether it was because of the gold, or because we felt so isolated, we took turns standing watch that night. I didn't want to be surprised by anyone, especially not the Sioux or Cheyenne, who may have been roaming the Hills.

During my watch, sometime after midnight, the good weather finally broke. I had moved out from under the big pine with my rifle, to have an unobstructed view of the valley. But "view" is the wrong word, since the moonless night was inky black. The only way I could distinguish anything was by looking up at the sparkling array of stars overhead. They seemed almost close enough to reach. The air was sultry and still—unlike the crisp night air we had experienced in the Hills so far.

The first indication I had of an approaching storm was a faint flicker of lightning just above the northwest rim of the valley. It was followed a few minutes later by another, brighter, flicker, and then a distant grumbling of thunder. The lightning began to come more and more frequently, and the thunder grew gradually louder. The longer blazes of approaching lightning revealed a towering thunderhead, billowing thousands of feet into the sky. Then the flashes flamed out, and the night was blacker than ever. While my eyes were still temporarily blinded, an earthshaking boom of thunder seemed to rattle the very boulder I was perched on. It was an awesome display of nature. Finally, the first faint puffs of air cooled my face as the wind from the storm reached down into the protected valley. I had seen summer storms like this before when sailing on Lake Michigan near my Chicago home. And the sight of one of these approaching storms had always given me a cold chill when I was out on the water. But now I watched with a relaxed fascination. However, about ten minutes later I was forced to take shelter under the pine tree as the storm broke over the valley in a fury of wind and rain. Thunder shook the hills and echoed back and forth in deafening crashes. Lightning and thunder followed each other without pause and the rain lashed down, driven by a gusting wind.

Wiley was sitting up and had wrapped his blanket and poncho around his shoulders, even though very little water was penetrating the thick downsweep of overhead boughs. Only a fine mist was blowing in on us from underneath. I had always avoided standing under trees in a thunderstorm, and this giant pine was at least a hundred feet high. But,

I reasoned, the chances of lightning's striking this particular tree were not any greater than the chances of its striking any of the hundreds of other trees in the area; the trees on the ridges were much higher.

The noise prevented any conversation, and we just looked at each other and shook our heads as the wind buffeted the branches over our heads and the continual flashes of lightning lit up the valley like noonday sun.

In an hour or so, the storm passed over, muttering and grumbling away. The two of us lay down on the almost-dry pine needles and slept until full daylight, secure in the notion that we were safe from any surprise attack from man or animal for the time being.

We were up the next morning at first light and went looking for our horse that had jerked out his picket pin when he was spooked by the thunder. We finally found both horse and mule grazing quietly near a rocky overhang at the head of the valley.

Then it was on to the all-important business of staking two adjacent claims along the most promising stretch of creek. While in the claims office in Deadwood, we had learned that most Black Hills claims ran three hundred feet in length and extended from rimrock to rimrock on either side. So we paced off six hundred feet—about two hundred steps for our two claims—and stacked up small piles of rocks to mark the boundaries. We found some birch bark and marked our names and the date with charcoal from our fire. Then we put these in two empty tin cans left from supper and embedded the can firmly in the rocks of our cairns.

Then we took a last look around to fix the place in our memories, so we would be sure to recognize this isolated valley the next time we saw it.

"What'll we name this place?" I asked as we rode up and out to return to our partners.

"Why name it?" Wiley wanted to know.

"We gotta call it something. And besides, this place may be as famous as Sutter's Mill some day."

"Okay. Let's see . . . How about Thunder Valley, since it stormed so hard on us last night?"

I couldn't think of any better name right off, so Thunder Valley it was.

When we got back to Curt and Cathy, we found that they had been drenched by the storm of the night before, and had spread all our gear out in the sun to dry. And their gold-hunting efforts had produced the same poor results as before. But they were elated by our good news when we showed them our dust.

"Looks like we're going to need some sort of shelter if we plan to stay awhile," Curt said. "Probably ought to ride back to town and see if we can get one of those big wall tents, and maybe a stove, too, since fall weather will be on us shortly."

The sky was clear, but the air was noticeably cooler since the storm.

"We need to file our claims, too," I put in.

"Why don't you and Wiley ride on back, then, since you know where the claims are. Let me give you a list of some supplies to pick up. Some of our flour and dried beans got soaked last night."

"Don't give those two prospectors up above us any indication that we'll be moving out to new diggins, or the direction," Wiley said.

"Okay. I don't know what they're getting, but they're sure hard at it. They've hardly looked our way."

"We'll wait for you here!" Curt yelled as we rode away.

"Be back some time tomorrow," I answered, pulling my horse's head around.

Since we were now riding instead of walking, the trip back to Deadwood seemed very short. We hit town about two in the afternoon, famished, since we hadn't taken time to eat anything all day. We turned our mounts into the livery with instructions for a rubdown and feed, and then headed straight for the Grand Central and a big meal.

Thus fortified, we stopped by the mining district claims office and recorded our claims for two dollars each, describing and locating on a wall map as best we could where they were located.

Then it was on to a dry goods store. We picked out a big white canvas tent, similar to those used by cavalry officers. It would be plenty big for the four of us, and, rolled up, it was also very heavy. We bought a small, bottomless, sheet-iron stove and three joints of stovepipe to go with it, then made arrangements to pick them up the next day.

"Damn! Look at these prices!" Wiley complained as we made our next stop for groceries. "They've gone up just in the last few days. I know prices are usually high in these gold camps, but this is ridiculous!"

"It costs a lot to freight this stuff in," the storekeeper reminded him calmly.

"But look at this," Wiley said, picking up a small sack. "A dollar a pound for Arbuckle's coffee? Seventy-five cents a pound for bacon? Two dollars a dozen for eggs? Sixty dollars for a hundred pounds of flour?"

"My margin of profit isn't that much," the storekeeper defended himself. "And I need to make a living, too, just as much as the men out on the creeks. They need me, and I need them. Besides, if you think this is high, just you wait until this winter, when our supplies are cut off. I expect prices to double and triple."

Still grumbling, Wiley paid for our supplies with some of our remaining greenbacks, so as to take advantage of the five percent discount.

"C'mon, let's haul this stuff to the hotel and then go get a drink," Wiley said disgustedly. "Whiskey's only twenty-five cents a glass," he said over his shoulder for the benefit of the unperturbed storekeeper.

We lugged the food in burlap sacks down the street and rented our old room at the Merchants Hotel, and then made a beeline for the Golden Eagle Saloon.

Our old friend Burnett was at his usual position behind the bar. In place of his broken front window, he had a solid wooden shutter that was hinged at the top so it could be swung up open and hooked to the roof of the board-walk to admit some light and air.

"Works pretty well," he told us when we inquired about it. "Those swinging doors let in the outside air, anyway, and we aren't bothered much with flies and mosquitoes here in the Hills. I just drop it and latch it when we close, which ain't too often."

Wiley ordered whiskey, and Burnett drew me off a foamy mug of draft—and we told him in low voices about our success at prospecting. I was a little hesitant at first about mentioning it to anybody, for fear of starting a rush in that direction—even though our claim was safely recorded. But the big bartender was a man I trusted instinctively. We didn't even reveal to him the exact location, although it was on public record in the claims office, had he wanted to check. He congratulated us and said, "I told you there was gold in that area if anyone had the guts to go after it. See any Indians?"

"Not a sign of one."

"I'll wager they saw you, although the army may have scared 'em off for the time."

"I imagine our gold will still be there when we get back."

"Oh, I'm sure the gold will be. The Sioux care little or nothing for that. But your partners may not be there; the Indians are more interested in white scalps."

Wiley and I exchanged glances. How much of this was exaggeration, and how much truth?

We refilled our drinks and had just sat down at a table to talk when the bat wing doors flew open and a little boy popped in. I couldn't have been more surprised if a leprechaun had suddenly appeared in our midst.

"Hi there, K.J. Haven't seen you around in the last few days," Burnett said, obviously greeting an old friend.

"Oh, I've been busy running errands and stuff," the boy replied.

"Gonna dance for us?" Burnett asked.

"If you want me to."

"What about it, boys?" Burnett called out to the two dozen or so men who were playing poker and faro. They voted their unanimous approval with a chorus of yells.

Whereupon, three or four of the men got up and pushed back the tables and chairs to clear a space on the wooden floor. The boy sat down and rummaged in a canvas pack he was carrying, brought out a scuffed pair of shoes with metal taps on them, and quickly changed his high-top shoes for these. Then with no hesitation, he jumped up and threw himself into a dance that was fast and furious. The taps rattled expertly on the wooden floor as he pivoted and stomped, swinging his arms. There was no accompanying music, but as he got warmed up, the men began to clap in unison in time to the beat. Finally, after three or four minutes, the clapping dissolved into applause and yells of approval, and coins began to rain down around him and roll on the planks. When he finished with a flourish, panting and sweating, the men broke into a wild cheer, and one of them grabbed him and lifted him up to sit on the bar while another gathered up his coins.

"You oughta see him when our piano player is here at night," Burnett said quietly to us as we crowded around the boy.

"Who is this kid, anyway?" I asked him.

"We all call him K.J. Don't know much about him. He dances in a lot of the saloons around here and the customers love him; he's good for business."

"Where does he live?"

Burnett shrugged. "Here, there, and everywhere. Runs errands and holds horses for tips. Hits the back doors of the restaurants for meals. Don't know where he sleeps."

"His name's KayJay?"

"It's his initials. Never heard him called anything else." He reached over and cut the boy a slice of dark yellow cheese from a wedge at the end of the bar and handed it to him while the boy talked to some of the men.

The boy could not have been over eight or nine years old and was scarcely four and a half feet tall, with a stocky, solid build. He had a mop of dark brown hair that nearly covered his ears and reached the collar of his faded plaid shirt. He had a short nose and a rather round face with alert, animated dark eyes and flashing white teeth. The pants he wore were obviously homemade and a little too long for him, since he had to roll them up a couple of turns. They were held up by suspenders.

His whole appearance was clean, threadbare, and merry.

The men were drifting back to their card games, and K.J. hopped down from the bar, wiping his hands on his pants and chewing the last of the cheese. The silver coins jingled in his pocket.

"Thanks, Burnett," he said cheerfully and with a familiarity that seemed out of place for one of his years. "I may be back tonight."

"Where do you live, boy?" Wiley asked him as he started out.

He looked up at us pleasantly. "Oh, around," he replied noncommittally.

"Don't you have any parents?"

He shrugged. "Naw." His nonchalance seemed rather affected. "I gotta go."

But Wiley's curiosity was not satisfied. He lounged out beside the boy, and I went too. "You must live someplace," Wiley said as we moved along.

"I stay with Missus Hayes most of the time," K.J. finally admitted. I could see that it was inconceivable to Wiley that a child like this could be completely on his own.

"Who's Missus Hayes?"

"She's an old lady who lives back up on the hill above town. She sells fruits and vegetables and stuff. Everybody knows her. She's nice."

"How old are you?"

"Ten," he replied promptly and with pride.

"Oh, c'mon, now. You don't look like you're over eight or nine."

"I'm ten," he insisted.

"You're a good tap dancer. Where'd you learn to do that?"

"Look, mister, I gotta go," he repeated, eyeing us suspiciously and sidling away. He reminded me of a wild animal shying away from human contact. Then he turned and broke into a run, darting across the street just ahead of a team and wagon.

"Amazing," Wiley muttered under his breath. He shook his head. "I can't imagine a kid like that living by his wits without any parents or guardian in a remote place like this. Wonder how he came to be here?"

"Beats me," I replied.

We went back to our hotel and rested an hour or so before going to supper. When we came back out, about six thirty, we saw a crowd spilling off the boardwalk and into the street around the Wells Fargo office.

"What now?"

"Maybe they're still riled up about that robbery a few days ago."

I didn't reply, but I knew instinctively there was more trouble coming.

CHAPTER 7

The giant Wells Fargo Company had moved into Deadwood early and was competing with a line called the Northwestern Express, Stage, and Transportation Company, which optimistically advertised on its oversized sign that it sold through tickets to Bismarck and all large eastern and Canadian cities, in addition to such unlikely places as Hamburg, Glasgow, Liverpool, "and all points in Europe." But it was the Wells Fargo Company that had the size and the reputation for dependability—a reputation that was beginning to suffer, we found when we crossed the street to its offices and stage depot. Adjacent to its stables, the unimposing glass-fronted office supported a wooden false front above it. This white false front was emblazoned by dark green block letters one- and two-feet high, reading:

WELLS FARGO & CO.
OVERLAND MAIL
AND
EXPRESS OFFICE

A smaller sign, about one foot by two, hanging near the front door, announced that the same building housed the Western Union Telegraph Office.

It took us a few minutes to wiggle our way through the tightly packed crowd and get inside the office next to the counter.

"All right, all right. Calm down! I know all of you have sustained losses," the harried express agent behind the counter was shouting above the noise. He was a blond young man with wire-rimmed spectacles and a neat,

reddish-brown mustache. He was wearing a natty dark
suit with a goldstone watch fob hanging from the pocket
of his tattersall vest. He was perspiring freely and mop-
ping his face with a handkerchief. The close air in the
room was made even worse by the crush of humanity in
the confined space.

"Wells Fargo has always reimbursed any losses on its
line. You know the company's good for it!" he was yelling, barely making himself heard as far as the front door.
"If you'll just bring me your receipts one at a time . . .
line up, line up. I can't talk to everyone at once."

"Hell, winter's coming on, Chuck!" a man behind me
yelled. "I can't afford to wait several weeks or months
for the company to refund my money from the home
office in San Francisco. I'll have to go outside and come
back in the spring."

The express agent called Chuck tried again, but his
voice was getting hoarse. Finally, he shrugged impotently
and let his hands fall to his sides, for his entreaties seemed
to be having no effect on the agitated crowd. He looked
over at Wiley and me, and since we were close at hand
and were two of the few who weren't berating him, he
said, just loud enough for our ears, "Most of these people
didn't have over an ounce or two of gold apiece on that
shipment. About a dozen shippers account for the rest."

"Another holdup?" I asked.

He nodded glumly. "Yeah."

"How much this time?"

"About twenty-five thousand dollars."

"Whew!"

"It wasn't any fortune, but it adds up in a hurry."

"I need my money! I was sending that gold to my
family back East. My wife and kids will be evicted from
the house!" shouted another man who had just gotten his
head inside the door.

"Hell, Frank, if you were concerned about your family's
income, you wouldn't be out here prospecting for gold!"
the Wells Fargo agent shot back, turning slightly red in
the face.

His retort didn't slow up the ranting of the crowd,

which was composed mainly of roughly dressed miners, with a sprinkling of white-shirted, dark-tied men who could have been merchants or bankers or even gamblers.

"Anyone killed this time?" Wiley asked.

"No, thank God," the agent replied.

Suddenly the roar of a shotgun just outside on the unroofed boardwalk split the noise of the crowd. The shouting died quickly to a mumble and then quieted altogether as the sheriff elbowed his way into the room, double-barreled shotgun braced on his hip and held high.

He was a short, stocky man in his mid-forties, wearing a high-crowned white hat and a cowhide vest over a pale blue shirt. He was sandy-haired and blue-eyed, with shaggy brows and a heavy, drooping mustache that was streaked with silver and stained on its lower edges with tobacco juice. The strong nose showed a fine tracery of red veins. I sized him up as a strong-willed, hard-drinking man who, at the moment, was all business.

"Okay, now!" he bellowed, glaring around him. "If any of you men have any legitimate business with Mister Bundy here, you just line up single file and he'll accommodate you."

He turned and glanced at Chuck Bundy, who was sagging against the counter, and he also looked up at the wall clock behind him. It read 6:47.

"On second thought," the sheriff resumed, "it's past suppertime. This office is closed for business as of now. It'll open on schedule at . . ." He turned and looked his question at the agent.

"Eight o'clock," Bundy replied tiredly.

"Eight A.M." shouted the sheriff. "Everybody clear out of here now. Go on. There's nothing can be done about it tonight, anyway. A posse's already out trying to pick up their trail."

"That posse'll be lucky if they can find their way back to town," somebody grumbled. The crowd mumbled and muttered and seemed reluctant to leave, but none of them was willing to argue with the sheriff's logic or his shotgun. They began to disperse, and drifted away in twos and threes.

"Thanks, Ben," Bundy said with relief. "Now for some food. It's been a long day."

"I'll bet," the sheriff replied. "C'mon. I haven't eaten either. If you're eating out, I'll join you." As they turned toward the door, they noticed Wiley and me still standing there. "Whata you two want?" the sheriff demanded.

"Just a little information, sheriff," I spoke up before Wiley had a chance to say anything. "We're not here to file any claims against the company or anything. But we might be bringing some dust here for smelting and shipping soon, and we just want to find out what's been going on." I held the door open for the two of them and Wiley to pass outside. "We've been out on the creeks and just came in town today," I explained.

Bundy took a ring of keys from his pocket and locked the door, and the four of us started down the boardwalk. The sheriff eyed us up and down, but apparently had no reason to think we were other than what we claimed, so he unbent a little. "You haven't even seen a newspaper?" he asked.

"No. We just got in this afternoon, and haven't had time to do anything but tend to business."

"Well, if you plan to ship some gold, this will shortly become your business," the sheriff said, shifting the short shotgun into the crook of his arm and pushing his hat back from his forehead. "Believe it or not, this morning makes the eighth stage to be robbed in about six weeks. Every one of 'em was outbound to Cheyenne, and every one of 'em was carryin' a shipment of gold to the railroad."

"Does every stage that leaves out of here going south have gold aboard?" Wiley asked.

"No. Not all of them. That's the thing about it. Wells Fargo has two stages a week going south, and one north; and Northeastern has three north and one south each week," Bundy replied.

"Hold it a minute," the sheriff said, and ducked inside his small office we were just passing. He was back in a second minus the shotgun.

"Any of the inbound stages been robbed?" I asked.

"Only two. Whoever's doing it knows that there's nothing coming in except passengers and mail. About the only thing they'd get there would be the personal effects and money of the passengers."

"Have any of the southbound stages been robbed that were not carrying treasure?"

"Not any of ours. Northwestern had one hit, but I think they'd put out the news that it had gold aboard."

"Any idea who's doing it?" I asked.

"Well, we've got some theories, and it won't be long before those gunmen are run down," the sheriff answered with an air of mysterious importance.

Bundy chuckled. "Come on now, Ben. You don't have any more idea who's behind this than the rest of us. I'm not saying you're not trying. I wouldn't have your job for anything, but we might as well admit it—we just don't have any leads."

"Humpf!" the sheriff snorted through his mustache without replying, and reached for a twist of tobacco in his vest pocket.

"Oh, by the way, I'm Charles Bundy," the express agent said, thrusting out his hand to us. "And this is our sheriff, Benjamin Pierce."

The sheriff nodded, but didn't offer his hand.

"I'm Matt Tierney, and this is Wiley Jenkins."

"Nice to know you."

"Are these gold shipments common knowledge?" Wiley asked.

"Pretty much so. There's so much gold coming out of the Hills just now that pretty nearly every stage that leaves out going south is likely to be carrying a full strongbox."

"Has the company tried using fake shipments or anything?"

"Oh, sure, we've tried lots of things. We've sent the gold out by wagon in the middle of the night, and they got it; we tried holding the gold until we had enough to melt it into one huge six-hundred-pound ingot, but the robbers showed up with a wagon, just as though they were expecting something heavy, and managed to haul it off. We found the wagon a few days later, burned, and no sign of the gold. We even used a special cast-iron box and bolted it to the floor of the coach, but they showed up with some of this new stuff called blasting gelatin— a helluva lot more explosive than black powder—and just blew the floor out of the stage and carried away the box still bolted to part of it. Then we even cast a gigantic gold and silver ingot that weighed over thirteen hundred pounds. Didn't think any gang of robbers could lift that."

"What happened?"

"Well," Bundy shook his head ruefully, "we outfoxed ourselves. The stage hit a big rut, and the jolt, along with all that weight, broke the thoroughbraces and the frame of the coach. We had a tough time just getting it back here so we could smelt it down again. Had to cut it in four pieces to haul it."

I laughed.

"Sounds like an inside operation," Wiley said.

"We've explored that idea, too, but so far haven't come up with anything. I'm only certain of one thing."

"What's that?"

"That *I'm* not the one who's behind it."

"Still sounds like an inside job," Wiley insisted.

"The way you two are asking questions, how do we know you're not mixed up in it?" the sheriff said.

"Don't they leave any sort of clues? Aren't the posses able to track them?" I asked Bundy, ignoring Pierce's comment.

"Sometimes it's just a lone bandit, sometimes two, and other times four or five. They seem to know just what's needed to get the job done. They change their locations of the robberies. One time they were even waiting inside the first swing station and had tied up the stock tenders."

"I know. We were in town when that one happened," Wiley said.

"Anyway," Bundy continued, "I've even been on some of the posses. And usually the trail either splits up after a few miles, or it disappears when they ride up into the granite hills, where only an Indian could have a chance of trailing them."

"What are you going to do?" I asked.

"We've got a few ideas that I can't talk about right now."

"Will you have to stop shipping gold?"

"Never. Wells Fargo has a reputation to protect. And that certificate on my office wall tells the world I'm their official representative here." There was no mistaking the set of the young man's jaw. I had no doubt he would engage the robbers in hand-to-hand combat if he got the chance.

"I'm talking about them as though they were all one group," he continued in a softer tone that reflected his bewilderment. "I have no idea who 'they' are. They may not be all one gang. It may be several individuals, or groups of individuals operating independently." He waved his arm in a sweeping gesture. "Hell, these hills are full of the meanest, orneriest scum you've ever seen. They just naturally migrate to these boom towns before the law gets really established. They've probably been run out of half the camps in California, Nevada, and Montana."

"Yeah. I've seen some of them," I said. "They must sleep all day and raise hell all night. A lot of them look like they'd cut your throat for a ten-cent piece."

At this point we reached the restaurant Bundy and Pierce had been heading for. I thanked the agent for the information, and Wiley and I clomped on down the walk to our favorite dining room at the Grand Central Hotel.

We stuffed ourselves with another good meal.

"Sure puts bacon and beans in the shade—along with pony meat," Wiley remarked, picking his teeth as we strolled outside. "Wouldn't mind eating like that from now on."

"If that gold pans out like I hope it will, you can afford to buy a lot of good meals—even at these prices."

"You think we'll have trouble getting it to Cheyenne?"

I shrugged. "We won't have to worry about that for a while, until we accumulate enough to make it worthwhile."

"That shouldn't be long, judging from the dust we were washing out the other day."

"Well, Mother Nature can be mighty fickle sometimes.

We'd better play it pretty close to the vest and not go making any big plans until we see what happens. But if we have enough to ship to Cheyenne, we'll get it there one way or another, if we have to haul it ourselves."

"It might be worth our while to volunteer to help that 'friendly' sheriff and the posse," Wiley suggested.

I eyed him sideways. "You've sure changed since I met you last spring," I ventured, hoping he wouldn't take offense. "You were only interested in looking out for yourself then. Never wanted to get involved in any causes."

"Still don't," he answered shortly, staring straight ahead. "Just thinkin' about protecting our own interests. I'm not fond enough of hard labor to sweat days or weeks shoveling and sluicing to let some damned masked coward with a gun walk off with it all for free."

"Well, at least you said 'our' interests. Maybe there's hope for that selfish heart of yours yet." I grinned at him.

His handsome, boyish face relaxed into a slight smile. "You know, I wouldn't let anyone but you or Cathy or Curt say that to me and get away with it. But maybe I have changed a little this summer, with all that's happened to me."

It was about the closest I had heard him come to letting down his constant defense.

"What time is it?" he asked, abruptly changing the subject.

"Don't rightly know. Sure miss my watch. Have to see if I can find a watchmaker in town." I looked around at the deepening darkness. The street along the bottom of the deep gulch was partially lighted by the yellow lamplight spilling from the open saloon doors, dance halls, and gambling dens up and down Main Street. "I'd guess about eight. Why?"

"Thought I might have a drink or two and try my luck at a little poker or faro. Maybe even try a little roulette."

I'm sure he couldn't see my raised eyebrows in the darkness. "You know the house has all the odds, even in a straight game?"

"Yeh, but that only gives me more incentive to beat 'em."

"As I recall, you were a little short on cash from 'bucking the tiger' when we first met in Cheyenne. And that was the reason you gave for signing on with the Third as a mule packer."

"That was part of the reason," he acknowledged, stopping on the sidewalk to rake a wooden match against the building and light a slim cigar. When he had it going well, he tossed the match into the street, and all I could see of him was the glowing end of his smoke. "Besides," he continued, "when were you appointed my guardian?"

I had feared he would take it that way. "Okay, okay. I'm not trying to tell you what to do. Just don't get drunk and start bragging about our claim or where it is. I'd like to get it pretty well worked out, or find out if it leads to something big before a whole damn stampede comes thundering out there."

"Don't worry."

"You bet I'll worry, but there's nothing I can do about it. I'm going to have a beer and go back to the hotel. I haven't slept in a real bed since last May, and I plan to get in a lot of rest tonight. Don't wake me up when you come in."

CHAPTER 8

"You're not saying much this morning," I chided Wiley as we rode out of Deadwood the next morning. He was astride the mule with our big tent rolled up and tied behind him. The rest of our supplies were packed on the horse with me. It was a warm day, and sultry, with no wind, and we were letting the animals walk along slowly.

Wiley gave me a pained look and didn't reply.

I chuckled. "Ah well, nothing in life is free."

He still said nothing, and I knew his hangover was fairly severe. It was too bad he wasn't in any condition to enjoy the morning. Even though the weather was coming on to be uncomfortably warm, we rode in shadow much of the time, the scent of pine was fresh, and birds cheered the day.

"Did you lose all your dust?"

"I didn't lose it; I spent it."

"On roulette?"

"Didn't do much gambling. Came out a little on the short end of that, but I had a little more to drink than I intended."

"I figured that." I knew how bad he must be feeling, with a bad head and queasy stomach, so I didn't rub it in. But he seemed to have brightened up somewhat.

"Met a girl."

"Oh, ho! That's where your money went."

"Yeh, most of it," he admitted absently, his face showing a faraway look.

"Nice, huh?"

"Beautiful."

"Well, tell me about her."

"She works in Burnett's place. About five-foot-two, short, dark hair, nice smile, and a great figure. I'd bet she's not over twenty. She's from Cincinnati."

"She doesn't double as one of Myra's girls, does she?" As soon as the words left my mouth, I knew I had said the wrong thing. He started to reply, bit back the words, started again, and finally choked out a "No," and let it go at that.

I looked ahead and pretended not to notice. "Sounds like a doll. You going to see her again?"

"First chance I get."

He fell silent once more, and I gladly let the subject drop as thoughts of my own girlfriend in Chicago swept into my mind. A tall, blonde secretary in my old newspaper office. What had she been doing all summer? Whom had she been seeing? She probably wouldn't even know yet that I wasn't coming back. Or at least not back to work there. Would she even care when she found out? Unlikely. She had probably forgotten all about me already in search of more promising prospects. It was not a flattering thought, but I had to be realistic. I think I had impressed her as a confirmed bachelor—in my early thirties, with a good job, and yet showing no signs of settling down. But nobody married young in Ireland, and this custom of taking one's time had been impressed on me from childhood. I let out an audible sigh and turned my mind to things at hand.

"What day is this, anyway?" I asked.

Wiley gave me a puzzled look. "You know, I really don't have any idea of the day of the week or the day of the month."

"I've completely lost track, too. I'm pretty sure we're still in September, but that's all I'm sure of. I know we've been mighty busy, but it's a shame when Sunday's just like every other day of the week."

"Why? You miss your day of rest? You can rest any time you want to now."

"Almost like we're not civilized anymore," I answered.

"How can you honor the Lord's day when you don't even know when it is?"

"Every day is the Lord's day, whether anybody wants to admit it or not," he said with a reflective insight that surprised me. I started to ask him what he meant, but instead just said, "I didn't know you were a religious man."

"Not as much as I should be, I guess," he replied, "but I had a pretty strict upbringing. And I've been rebelling against it ever since I left home."

"Nobody out here to tell you what to do."

"I know, but old habits die hard," he said. He looked up at me, running his fingers through his wavy brown hair. He had slung his hat by its lanyard over the saddle pommel. "I suppose you're Catholic, being from southern Ireland and all."

"Born and bred," I replied. "But I haven't seen hide nor brick of a priest or a church since I left Chicago."

"We haven't seen much of anything but soldiers, horses, and Indians for months—until we reached Deadwood. And if Deadwood has a church of any kind, I sure haven't spotted it."

"It's a little tough to spot a church from inside the Golden Eagle," I murmured.

For the first time that morning, he grinned. "Don't make me laugh," he begged, "it jars my head."

"Getting back to women," I said, "maybe it's time you latched onto a good girl, got married, and settled down."

"I don't notice you rushing into the arms of marital bliss," he retorted. "And you're a lot older than I am."

"Curt's about my age," I defended lamely, "and he's still single."

"He's been in the army or college ever since he was in his late teens. Probably hasn't had much chance to meet any good women."

"Looks like he's interested in your sister, Cathy."

"She's pretty independent. But I hope he doesn't lead her on and then drop her."

"He's been stuck on her for quite a while. If I know

Curt, he wouldn't do that unless he had some serious intentions."

"Curt Wilder's one helluva nice fella. Wouldn't mind at all having him for a brother-in-law. He and I see eye-to-eye on this business of war. Never would've thought it when I first met him."

"Well, if this gold claim keeps on producing, none of us will have to worry about how we'll make a living for a while."

We fell into silence for a few minutes as my mind conjured up what life might be like with unlimited golden wealth. I guessed Wiley was probably thinking the same thing. But then maybe he was just savoring the silence and nursing his hangover, trying to keep the motion of the walking mule from making him sick.

"You know, that kid was in the saloon again last night," he said unexpectedly.

"What kid?" I asked, not following his jump in thought.

"What's his name—K.J.? Yeh, that's it. Boy, he's a good little tap dancer. You should have seen him with that piano player. They put on a real show. They had the whole place stomping and yelling for more."

"Did you find out any more about him or where he came from?"

"Well, Jenny told me—"

"Who's Jenny?"

"Oh, I thought I told you. She's the girl I met. Anyway, she told me those initials stand for Kenneth Joseph."

"No last name?"

"She didn't know it. Nobody seems to. She said he stays with an old lady named Hayes, just like he told us. It seems this Missus Hayes is an old widow who sells vegetables and fruit and takes in homeless kids and derelicts—and also acts as a mother and place of refuge for any of the prostitutes in town. She also has a reputation as a sometime nurse and weather predictor. What she lacks in earnings from her produce stand, she makes up for in contributions from grateful people she helps."

"Sounds like she's all things to all people."

"Jenny says the old lady has an open door, a soft shoulder, and a big ear, not to mention heart."

"Think I'll look her up next time I'm in town; she sounds like a person worth meeting."

"Me, too."

"By the way, what's Jenny's last name?"

"Johnson."

"I like that name—Jennifer Johnson."

"You'd like it even more if you saw who's wearing it."

"I'll get you to introduce me next time we're in town."

In less than an hour more of easy riding, we were back with Curt and Cathy. They had found only slight traces of gold while we had been gone, so we helped them load up our gear, and Wiley, his hangover beginning to wear off, rigged two good packs, one for the mule and one for the horse.

"Want to say good-bye to our unsociable neighbors up the creek?" I asked Curt as we prepared to lead our loaded animals away. The prospectors were still hard at it in the edge of the trees.

"No, thanks."

"Then, Thunder Valley, here we come."

In order not to invite curiosity about our eventual destination, we led our animals out of the valley the same way we had first come in and made a wide detour of three or four miles around. It was extremely rugged terrain, and we had to backtrack several times to find a way up and over the steep ridges. Wiley and I nearly lost our bearings, and probably would have if it hadn't been for the sun, but finally we led the group to Thunder Valley. It was coming on to late afternoon, and the sun had long since dropped over the ridge, throwing this cool, green valley into shadow. It was a welcome relief from the heat of the day and our exertions of walking and climbing.

We selected a level spot near the head of the canyon to pitch our big tent. There was plenty of wood and grass nearby, and the stream that hid the gold also provided cold, clear water.

In the days that followed, we cut and trimmed logs

and built a foundation about two feet high around the
tent. We set up our iron stove and ran the pipe out the
small hole in the side. The stove served not only for
cooking, but also provided warmth, for a sharp autumn
chill was beginning to settle over the valley during the
nights. The tent was roomy enough to rope off and hang
blankets to give Cathy some privacy when required. We
occasionally roamed a few miles from Thunder Valley to
bring down a small deer to augment our larder and provide some variety of fresh meat to relieve the monotony
of bacon, beans, flapjacks, and dried fruit. The stream
in the valley was not large enough to contain any fish.

We discovered shortly after we settled in that the
amount of gold in the stream would justify building a
sluice box or rocker, but we had overlooked one vital
ingredient—lumber. There were plenty of trees around,
but we had no means of whipsawing them into green
lumber.

"I for one am sure glad we forgot to get a saw,"
Wiley said when we discovered our problem. "Have any
of you ever sawed a ten-foot log into planks?" he asked
rhetorically, looking around at us. "Well, I have. And it's
the most back-breaking, lung-searing, hand-blistering work
you can imagine. The log is usually laid over a pit or
across some kind of a brace above-ground. The man on
the lower end of the saw gets a faceful of sawdust in addition to everything else. That work makes double-jacking
contests look like playing fiddlesticks. Hell must be full
of crosscut saws."

"Okay, you made your point." Curt grinned. "Why
don't you take some of the dust we've accumulated and
go into the sawmill in town and buy enough lumber for
a good sluice and some nails to put it together? We'll
need some heavy screen and other stuff. We've already
got shovels. While you're there, why don't you see if you
can pick us up another pack mule."

"And stay out of trouble," Cathy warned him as she
saw her brother's eyes light up at the suggestion of returning to Deadwood.

But after some discussion, Curt decided he wanted to

go back to town also. So, not wanting to leave Cathy alone, we all set out for Deadwood after breakfast one morning. The sun hadn't yet shown its head over the valley rim to melt off the frost that was now becoming a nightly occurrence.

It took us about three hours to reach town again. I don't know whether it was because I was becoming used to the solitude of Thunder Valley, but the place seemed to be bursting with activity. The streets swarmed with people, and full stagecoaches were arriving and departing from both ends of town, at both the Wells Fargo depot and the Northwestern Company office. More frenzied building was going on during every daylight hour. The saloons and gambling dens never closed their doors, and Main Street was ablaze with light all night as well as all day. Lusty miners and travelers paid their money and bedded the girls upstairs at the Last Chance, the Red Rooster, the Union Brewery, and at least two dozen other places, while more thick-rolled and discreet businessmen and citizens called at Myra's Golden Bell and one or two other houses in town that catered to a more select, and often-washed clientele. Burnett's Golden Eagle was one of several places that didn't have its saloon girls doing double duty with the customers in another part of the building.

The whole town reminded me of nothing so much as a swarm of flies at the end of summer, who instinctively know their end is near and become a buzzing, biting nuisance. Such was Deadwood just before winter closed it down and isolated it from the outside world for several months.

And, incongruously, coming and going in the midst of all this commotion was a constant stream of the Chinese who operated the wash houses and several of the eating places. Their's was a plentiful business, and they worked hard, but they never mingled with the strange Caucasians whose laundry they did. They came and went with their padded clothing and long queues, their smooth Oriental faces showing no emotion. I wondered what they thought about or talked about among themselves. Were they trying to earn enough to go back to China and retire? Were they trying to earn passage for relatives to join them here in this alien white civilization? The inscrutable faces and the language barrier hid the answers. Wiley and Cathy both told me they had seen them in many of the earlier boom towns, including Virginia City. Many of them had been brought in to provide labor for the building of the Central Pacific Railroad in the sixties.

We tied our horse and our mule to a hitching rail in the middle of town, and before we could make a move in any direction or my ears become accustomed to the din, our attention was arrested by the shouting of a drummer haranguing a crowd some ways down Main Street. Since we were in no particular hurry, we drifted toward the sound.

When we reached the fringe of the crowd that was packed fifteen or twenty deep around him, we could hear and see the man who was standing on the tailgate of his wagon. The ornate wagon was drawn up near the side of the street to let the traffic pass. The rig was tall and enclosed, with a sliding curtain screening the interior of the wagon as the salesman gave his pitch. He was a tall, well-built man who looked to be in his late forties. He wore a swallowtail coat of gray with a velvet collar, and a gaudy red vest strung with a heavy gold watch chain. He had laid aside his silk top hat, revealing a head of magnificent silver hair. It was swept back in waves that caught the sun, and was matched by a full, well-trimmed gray mustache that set off a somewhat florid complexion —a complexion that was made even redder by his exertions.

"—and so, ladies and gentlemen, in the absence of doctors and medical men, you need to take extra care of your health, especially here in this climate of changing extremes. Winter is coming on. The chill of exposure, getting rundown, perhaps not eating the proper food. In these crowds, no telling what types of diseases may be spread—" He swept his arms around as he spoke, his voice growing a little hoarse in his efforts to make himself heard above the street noise.

"Well, set your minds at ease," he continued. "I have here the elixir that will allow you to put the state of your health out of your minds and concentrate on what you came here to find. I have chosen this remote settlement to introduce to you men and women of the West the exact blend of herbs and secret ingredients that it took me, Doctor Floyd Mortimer, a doctor of the sciences, ten years to develop. It will not only prevent most illnesses by strengthening and enriching your blood, but will lessen the symptoms and promote quick recovery from biliousness, the grippe, ague, mountain fever, carbuncles and corns, disorders of the liver and stomach. It will invigorate bodies tired from toil and"—he winked broadly—"from too much play.

"The medical profession sought to induce me to keep this amazing tonic for the exclusive use of doctors. But I rejected their pleas. I have always had a compassion for the common man. Why should this elixir of life, which I, after years of experimenting, finally discovered, be secreted in the halls of medical science and hospitals? I ask you: Why not bring it directly to the people? Why not, indeed! Not only is my tonic effective, as a curative, but it is absolutely safe when taken as directed. It requires no physician to dispense it."

He held up a square, pint-sized bottle whose label was covered with printing.

"And so, it is with the greatest of pleasure in serving mankind, that I offer this to you today."

"How much?" someone in the crowd shouted.

"I'm coming to that, sir, I'm coming to that. Since this is the very first place in this expanding western country that I've offered my amazing tonic, I'm prepared to offer it to you for the absolutely unbelievable price of only two dollars per bottle. Think of it! Only two dollars to put you in the pink and to stave off all the many ailments that flesh is heir to—"

"The only thing that stuff will cure is your pocketbook, if you can sell enough of it!" a voice beside me shouted

as the speaker paused to take a breath. It was Wiley. He
grinned at my surprised look.

"Always did like to needle these snake-oil salesmen,"
he said.

"Ah, my young friend, you know not whereof you
speak," the bombastic one continued smoothly. "The
pharaohs, in all their wisdom, sought such a cure and
failed. The medieval alchemists merely sought to change
base metals into gold, and, of course, they failed. Even
had they succeeded, mankind would not have benefited
as much as it will now from this discovery. And discovery
it is!" he shouted, regaining his volume. "Rather than an
invention. It was there in nature all the time, only awaiting
the genius of the scientific mind to combine the right
elements. It's an even greater discovery than the harness-
ing of steam for the good of all—"

"Will that stuff cure fatigue of the ears?" someone
shouted. A ripple of laughter swept the assembly.

"You, sir, will you be the first to try a bottle?" the
drummer shot back, singling out his heckler. The heckler
dropped his eyes from the pointing finger and looked
embarrassed. His friends laughed and shoved him forward.

"Come, come, sir, show these good people that you
care more for your good health than you do for all their
laughter. Distinguish yourself by being the first to purchase a pint of Doctor Mortimer's Elixir. And, sir, you
look like a sporting man to me," the drummer yelled,
moving in for the kill on the heckler, who was still being
shoved forward in the crowd.

"Brother, is he a sporting man!" shouted one of his
friends. "You oughta see him when he gits likkered up!"
Another ripple of laughter.

"I'll make you a deal," the drummer was intoning.
"If you try a bottle of this, and don't feel better in one
hour"—he thrust up one forefinger for emphasis—"then
you bring the empty bottle back to me and I'll give you
not only your money back, not only double your money
back, but *triple* your purchase price back—six dollars

refunded! Now, sir, you can hardly beat a deal like that!"

There was murmur of assent in the crowd, and by this time the heckler was at the tailgate of the wagon, digging in his pocket for money.

I edged around to the side a little so that I could see the wagon. It was a lightweight rig pulled by a single sorrel stallion of beautiful proportions. The wagon was new, and the varnished spokes almost glistened under a light layer of dust. The wagon body and the enclosed upper portion were painted a deep maroon, and were inscribed with elegant gold letters which advertised DOCTOR FLOYD MORTIMER, D.S. of BOSTON, and went on to tout the curative powers of his "Elixir of Life," which, if one could believe the testimonials, had been the very savior of some of the titled heads of Europe, on whom it had evidently been tested.

"Well, he's got 'em suckered now," Wiley said as the curious crowd, now unafraid to be seen buying the stuff— since someone else had broken the ice—pushed up close to make their purchases.

"In order for him to make a guarantee like that, the stuff's probably half alcohol," Curt remarked as several eager customers were uncorking their bottles and sampling the contents.

"Easy now, folks, easy!" Mortimer yelled with a half-smile as he made change. "Read the instructions on the label, or it won't have its most efficacious effects."

I got the distinct feeling he could not care less what was done with the medicine once it left his hands.

"You mean you're not going to buy a bottle?" Curt asked Wiley in mock seriousness as we drifted away.

"No, thanks. Burnett dispenses the only kind of medicine I'm interested in."

"Yes, and you're going to ruin your health drinking so much," Cathy said in a wistful, rather than a scolding, voice.

"Wiley works on the theory that if a little is good, then more is better," I offered, only half jokingly.

"Okay, okay," Wiley answered. "A little nip of John Barleycorn now and then is good for the blood."

"A little, yes. That's what Doctor what's-his-name—Mortimer—claims for his elixir, too."

"Well, let's be after some wood and tools," Curt said, abruptly changing the subject. "We need to get that sluice box built and working; winter won't wait forever."

CHAPTER 9

In spite of the fact that Curt wanted to get back to the claim before dark, we were delayed at the mill getting our lumber—and further delayed at the hardware, where crowds of new prospectors were overwhelming the clerks' ability to wait on them. By the time we had finished and had also bought another mule, the afternoon was far advanced, and Wiley argued successfully that we shouldn't start our long walk and ride back until the next morning. The rooms at the Merchants Hotel were all full, so we had to rent our lodgings from the International, a much more expensive hotel. Even at that, we were lucky to find a room at all, with the crowds of people in town. Apparently, the majority were either not staying in Deadwood, or the rooms were too high for most of the prospectors—who were fleeing the lingering effects of the Grant administration's financial panic.

I took advantage of the layover to take my watch, along with Curt's, to Rosenthal's Jeweler and Watchmaker, a new shop that had just opened since our last trip to town.

Wiley could hardly wait until supper was over to make a beeline for Burnett's place to wet himself down and to see Jenny again.

The days were growing rapidly shorter; the sun had long since disappeared behind the steep hills when we stepped out onto the boardwalk. It was almost dark. The traffic on the street was as heavy as it had been at midday, except that Floyd Mortimer's wagon was nowhere to be seen.

Wiley lighted a cigar and looked down the street at the two rows of lights that were glowing from the open doors of the saloons and dance halls like so many open furnaces.

"Gomorrah in the gulch," he remarked.

"An apt metaphor," Curt agreed.

The next day we were back on our claim in Thunder Valley, hard at work building our sluice. Even in a matter of a few hours the memory of the hive of Deadwood seemed somehow unreal.

"You feel okay, Wiley?" I asked as I came up to the creek bank where he was hammering the last nails into the side of the new sluice.

"A little rusty, but I'll be all right." He glanced at Curt and Cathy, who were preparing supper near our tent about fifty yards away. He didn't seem disposed to talk.

"Jenny's beautiful," I ventured, attempting to draw him into conversation. "She seems so young and innocent to be working in a saloon in a boom town like that."

"Yeah," he agreed. "But I'm wondering if she is."

"Is what?"

"Innocent."

"Oh?"

"Yeah. Just some little hints and clues I've picked up. I'm sure she's not aware she's giving them to me. It's depressing, but I guess I'm naive to expect her to be different from those other saloon girls."

"You really like her, huh?"

"Yeah. That's the hell of it. I guess I was just hoping that . . . maybe she was different . . . you know. I got so depressed and frustrated, I got drunk and went down to Myra's place last night. Helped some, but now I feel worse than ever."

"I guess a man's conscience never takes a day off. Come on to supper."

For the next two weeks everything was driven from our minds except the sluice, the stream, and the gold we could strain from it. It was hard, wet, back-breaking work from dawn to dark, with hardly time out to eat while we could still see to work. We had set the new sluice box in the stream near the head of Thunder Valley, and began shoveling dirt and gravel into it. We gradually moved the box downstream after a few days in each spot, and the cleanup each evening began to increase— $1.50, $2.50, $4.00, $5.50, $8.00, $13.00, $27.50, $29.00, $34.50, and one memorable day when we cleaned $76 worth of pure gold dust and grains out of the tail of our sluice—almost four ounces in a ten-hour day. At this pace we would never be rich, but it was more than enough to make expenses, and, more importantly, it kept our interest at a high pitch.

One morning, sometime in late October, we came out of our tent to a cold overcast and a wind blowing out of the north. Shortly after noon, it began to snow and continued all afternoon. It was not bitterly cold, so we went on working, cleaning up over forty dollars' worth of gold before we knocked off for the night. That night the tent shook with the gusts of wind and the snow drifted up around the log base. Our sheet-iron stove was stoked to capacity, but there were so many air leaks around the tent that we were still cold in our blankets before morning.

The sky was clear next day, and the sun rising on the sparkling white world nearly blinded us. The air warmed up, and the six inches of white covering began to melt rapidly.

We worked like squirrels all that day, knowing we were in competition with winter for the gold remaining in our creek. The days were growing rapidly shorter, cutting down on the number of daylight hours we had to work. We cut out everything else and did nothing but work, pausing only before dawn and after dark to eat. Our sleep became exhausted oblivion. Carelessly, we kept no guards or watches, leaving the warning of any approaching danger to our two braying mules. It was probably a foolish thing to do, but we had to make our stake while we could. And, I'll admit, the yellow metal was beginning to get a grip on my imagination and emotions. It was no longer just a practical thing with me, and I suspect the sirenlike lure was affecting the others as well, although we never discussed it.

About ten days of Indian summer followed our first snow, and we took advantage of it. Our buckskin pokes began to swell with dust and small nuggets. It became a ritual every night by the light of our lantern for us to take turns hefting the small sacks and guessing their weight, trying to estimate how much they had gained since the day before, calculating in our heads their approximate value.

Our guesses had reached eighteen hundred to two thousand dollars before we got our second snowfall. It started as a light rain in the midafternoon, and by dark was fine grains of snow. The wind was hardly blowing at all, but the air had a raw edge to it. We huddled in our tent that night, more silent than usual after supper, listening to the scratching of the half-frozen sleet pellets on the canvas. We hadn't bathed in over a week, begrudging the time away from our precious sluice, and we all looked dirty. Our faces were gaunt and our bellies flat from the many hours of manual labor we had been performing.

It was probably from being so run-down, and possibly from not having any of Dr. Mortimer's Elixir, that Wiley developed a hacking cough that night. When I woke up once to relieve myself outside, I could hear him tossing and turning in his blankets.

By daylight the snow was still falling straight down, and had developed into large, fluffy flakes. And Wiley was running a fever to go along with his cough. By silent, common agreement we didn't attempt to go outside or do any sluicing that day. We sat, wrapped in our coats and blankets, near the glowing stove and drank hot tea and coffee. At Wiley's insistence, we laced his black coffee with whiskey and sugar, but Curt was hesitant to do that, fearing it might make his condition worse. He gave in only after he had stoked Wiley with a good breakfast of flapjacks, maple syrup, and bacon.

Shortly after, Wiley rolled up in his blankets and was dead asleep again in a couple of minutes.

"What do you reckon's wrong with him?" I asked Curt as we looked at the sleeping form.

"Don't rightly know. Could be most anything. Exhaustion. Maybe some sort of mountain fever."

"Well, we have nothing to treat him with, even if we knew."

"Oh, yes we do," Cathy said. "We have love and concern. We can keep him warm and well fed. We'll let him sleep a lot. We can give him hot tea and hope the fever will break. And we can pray." Her eyes were bright with tears, but her voice was firm.

As she spoke, she was dipping a cloth into a pan of water, wringing it out and wiping her brother's flushed face.

I think all of us were glad for a day off from our prospecting. We spent the hours cleaning up our neglected tent, airing out our blankets, changing and washing our clothes. Curt hauled water from the creek in buckets and heated it on the stove. We also washed ourselves as best we could, and Curt and I shaved. I, for one, felt a hundred percent better after I had cleaned up.

Wiley slept off and on through the day. He was restless, and apparently dreaming, but he slept.

"I think I'll go back to Kentucky for a visit," Cathy announced as we were cooking supper late that afternoon. Curt and I stared at her with our mouths open. She didn't look up from pulling at some loose threads on her blanket.

"Why?" Curt asked finally.

She took a deep breath before she answered. "I've been thinking about it for some time. Wiley can come with me if he wants to. But I haven't been home in over a year, and I'm sure that none of the family knows about my father's death. On second thought, they may have heard about it through the New Hope Mining and Milling Company, where he worked. The company probably got the news from the official dispatches of the battle. In any event, we need to settle up his affairs if it hasn't already been done. We were his closest kin."

She looked at Wiley's clammy face where he lay sleeping. "I don't want him to die in this wilderness. And

I'm afraid that's what will happen if he stays. Of course, it's up to him what he wants to do. But I'd like to get him home for a visit, anyway."

"If you're going, you'd better not wait too long," Curt said, obviously disappointed. "The stages to Cheyenne will only be running on an irregular schedule from now on until winter shuts them down completely. And that probably won't be long."

"The first thing is to get Wiley well, or at least well enough to travel. That is, if he decides to go."

"Will you . . . will you be back in the spring?" Curt asked, as if he were afraid to voice the question.

"I might. I'm not sure at this point. Now that my father is gone—and I had been traveling with him—I need to decide what I'm going to do with myself."

At this point supper was ready, and no more was said on the subject. We fell to as though we hadn't eaten for days.

The snow continued that night and most of the next day. It stopped the second night, and the sky cleared, but it then grew bitterly cold. We had not bought any heavy winter clothes, and we spent a miserable night sleeping as close to our small sheet-iron stove as possible, while wrapped in everything we owned. The only good thing that happened was the two feet of drifted snow insulating our log foundation and the base of the tent prevented the rising wind from whipping in around the corners.

Wiley's fever rose during the night, and we took turns swabbing him with cool, wet cloths. He became delirious and mumbled and spoke unintelligibly, sometimes with his unseeing eyes wide open. Between caring for him and hauling wood from outside the tent to stoke our voracious stove, we got little sleep that night.

Sometime in the early morning hours, his fever broke in a flood of perspiration. We dried him off and wrapped him up again. About an hour after daylight he opened his eyes weakly and asked for something to eat. His handsome face was pale and covered with stubble, and his cheeks and eyes looked sunken. Cathy fed him hot broth and a small piece of corn bread, and he lapsed into another sleep, but this time he appeared to be resting comfortably.

All day the sun shone on the dazzling white snow, but the wind gusted bitterly, and little, if any, melting took place. Curt and I took turns breaking through the snow to tend the animals, who had found shelter under a rocky overhang at the head of the valley, about eighty yards from our tent. Here, what little snow had swirled underneath was shallow, and easily pawed away by the animals for the still-green grass beneath.

It was three more days before the weather moderated sufficiently to travel. It was muddy, and our stream was gushing full to overflowing, but more bare patches than snow patches were showing.

Wiley had recovered almost completely, although he still looked very thin. He was eating everything in sight and joking, so we knew he was his old self again. When Cathy proposed the trip home to him, he didn't have to weigh the decision for more than five minutes. He would go. He expressed some regret at leaving us, but the prospect of enduring one of the high plains winters the northern Hills were subject to appalled him even more.

The next day the thaw continued, with some sunshine and a temperature in the high fifties. The horse carried Cathy and Wiley double while Curt and I rode the mules, as we set out for Deadwood. We arrived there shortly after ten, and a drearier sight we could hardly have imagined. The weather had slowed activity in the town considerably, and just getting around was a major problem, since the main street was a quagmire of sticky gumbo.

Curt and I had decided to go down to Cheyenne on the stage with them to see them off on the Union Pacific. We needed a break ourselves, and we were all a little tired of looking at the Hills and Deadwood.

We turned our animals into the nearest livery stable to be grain-fed and cared for while we were gone, and then walked to the Wells Fargo office to buy our tickets.

"That'll be a hundred and twenty-three dollars each, one-way," the blond agent, Bundy, told us.

"Two one-way, and two round-trip," Curt said, pulling out one of our pokes to pay.

The agent weighed out nearly seven hundred dollars' worth of our hard-earned dust, wrote out our tickets, stamped them, and handed them over to us.

"If you're carrying any valuables or dust on your persons, I have to warn you that you do so at your own risk. The company assumes no liability for anything except express packages or bullion."

"Does that mean we're liable to get robbed?" Curt asked.

"We've had a few holdups," Bundy conceded. "We're able to take measures to protect treasure shipments, but we have no way of protecting passengers in the same way. We do everything we can to safeguard our passengers, of course," Bundy assured us, "but we must warn you that there is some risk involved."

"Hell, Bundy, you can level with us," I said. "Is there gold aboard this coach?"

He looked at me closely, and then a flicker of recognition crossed his face. "Oh, yes. You two were in here the last time we had a robbery."

"That's been three or four weeks. Is that the last time there was a holdup?" Wiley asked.

"That's the last time a treasure coach was held up," Bundy replied evasively.

"You didn't answer our question: Is there gold aboard this coach?"

"I'm sorry, but company policy now dictates that we cannot give out that information."

"Don't worry," a bewhiskered miner in the room said as he overheard the conversation. "If you see a lot of guards and outriders, you know there's gold aboard." He ambled on outside to prop a chair in the wan sunshine and work a fresh chew into his cheek.

"How long will it take us to get to Cheyenne?" I asked Bundy.

"You'll have to check with the driver. It's hard to maintain any kind of a schedule this time of year. Could be as little as two and a half days, on up to six days, depending on the condition of the roads and the weather."

"In that case, I think I'll get a little food to carry along."

"Oh, there is food available at the stations along the way," Bundy said.

"We've heard," Wiley replied, making a wry face.

Two more people came into the office, and the four of us went outside into the chilly air and started toward the nearest grocery store, being careful to stay on the sidewalk to avoid the gumbo of the street.

"How do you feel, Cathy?" I asked as she walked on ahead of me. "You look like you're a little fuller in the hips than you were yesterday." Her short doeskin jacket barely reached her hips.

She grinned at me over her shoulder. "I feel heavy. My thighs and hips sure didn't need any more padding."

"That's about the most expensive outfit you're ever likely to wear," her brother said.

Curt looked around to make sure we weren't being overheard. "That was a good idea of yours to sew that gold dust into thin strips up and down the inside of your pants," he told her. "Besides being inconspicuous, I doubt that any would-be robber would search a woman that close."

"I'm at least six pounds heavier," Cathy said. "My legs feel strange."

We bought a small block of cheese, some bread, and some canned oysters. Curt had a two-quart canteen of water slung over his shoulder.

We all had our warmest, and only, coats on. But we still shivered in the damp, chill air. Snow was still piled between the buildings and on the shaded hillsides. The only remaining green was provided by the firs and pines.

We stepped into Rosenthal's Jeweler and redeemed our repaired watches.

When we got back to the Wells Fargo office, the stock handlers were leading the six-horse hitch out into the street. They began tightening and adjusting the traces. The team had in tow a beautiful red Concord coach with gold trim and lettering. Across the top, above the windows,

were the words, *Wells Fargo & Co. Overland Stage*, and
on the door, above a symbolic white eagle with spread
wings, the words, *U.S. Mail*. The eight-foot high coach
appeared to have been recently washed and was gleaming
in its red paint and big yellow wheels, with its brassbound
lanterns on either side.

Only after I had pulled my eyes away from the grace-
ful curves of the coach did I notice the other passengers
waiting on the wooden boardwalk. Besides the four of
us, there was a miner with a full, bushy, salt-and-pepper
beard. He was dressed in heavy canvas overalls and a
blanket coat. A black hat was pulled low on his head,
effectively hiding the part of his face that wasn't already
covered by the beard.

The remaining passenger was a well-dressed man of
medium height who wore a thick, squared-off mustache
of dark brown that hid his mouth. He was wearing glasses
that were silver-rimmed, with lenses of an unusually large
size, compared to normal reading glasses. He had on a
black, medium-crowned hat with a rather narrow brim,
a white shirt and tie, a short overcoat of black wool that
reached only halfway between his waist and knees, and
stylish, polished boots. I took in all this in a casual sort
of way, trying not to be too obvious about it. The man
stood aloof, his overcoat thrown back and one hand
thrust into an inside pocket. He seemed a little agitated
as he paced a few steps back and forth on the boardwalk,
chewing on the ends of his mustache and occasionally
slipping out his watch to check the time.

Stacked on the edge of the walk were some small packages and boxes, a canvas mailbag, a leather valise, a
canvas sack tied at the top, and our own luggage in two
small canvas packs. After the driver had stowed all of this
except the mailbag in the rear boot and tied it shut, Agent
Bundy and the shotgun messenger came out the door,
carrying the familiar Wells Fargo green strongbox between them. They lifted it into the front boot. The mailbag was flung in after it.

I was surprised to see that the shotgun messenger was

none other than Sheriff Ben Pierce. He looked grim and businesslike as usual.

"Reckon he's working for the company now, or do you think they can't get anybody else to ride guard?" Wiley voiced my own question quietly to the four of us.

"Don't know," I replied. "He's still wearing his badge."

"Maybe this is a special run."

"Well, if that strongbox was full of gold, they're taking no pains to hide the shipment."

"It did look pretty heavy," Curt put in, "but it could be a decoy. I don't see anyone getting ready to escort us as outriders, as the oldtimer said they would."

"Okay, folks, let's get aboard. We're movin' out!" the driver called sharply as he stepped up on the hub and swung himself deftly onto the high box. The six of us climbed in, Curt holding the door for Cathy to go first. She sat facing forward between me and Curt, as we sat facing the miner, the well-dressed man, and Wiley opposite. Thank God we weren't crowded enough to have someone on the middle bench between us. Bundy slammed the door and signaled the driver.

I pulled out the watch I had just gotten back from Rosenthal's. It was 11:05.

Before I could even snap the case shut, the driver's shout came through the open windows, and a crack of his whip sent the team and coach lunging away toward Cheyenne.

CHAPTER 10

After the first flourish of leaving town, the horses settled into a trot, and the corduroy road kept us from getting bogged down in the soft gumbo. The wheels were spinning off a fine spray of mud and water past our windows, and the coach rocked fore and aft on its thick leather thoroughbraces as we wound down the valley. It had been a long time, I reflected, since I had reclined on red leather upholstery.

Wiley, sitting opposite me, still looked wan and weak. He just drew his coat closer around him against the draft and stared out at the passing scenery. The man next to him in the middle was the well-dressed, nervous passenger. He seemed oblivious to everyone else in the coach. The faraway look in his eyes denoted some problem I could only guess at. In spite of the presence of a lady, he pulled a long, slim cheroot from an inside pocket and struck a match to it, cupping his hand around the flame until it was well-lighted and glowing. The bearded miner was also silent, his hat pulled low over his face as he appeared to be almost dozing. Everyone seemed to be engrossed in his own private thoughts.

It was going to be a long, lonely winter in Deadwood for me without Cathy and Wiley. I felt I had known them for years, instead of the few short months that had passed since our lives became so intertwined. Curt, who never let his emotions show very much, must have been feeling an even greater sense of loss than I from Cathy's leaving. I could only guess at how close their relationship had grown, either emotionally or physically or both, in the weeks since we had deserted the Third Cavalry. If they

99

were contemplating marriage, I had gotten no wind of it. But then, I never was the type to pry into another man's or woman's personal affairs. My reporter's nose didn't lead me to inquire into affairs of the heart. But besides being good-looking and sometimes emotional, Cathy Jenkins was, above all, practical.

My thoughts drifted off Curt and Cathy, and I began to wonder what was happening on my old newspaper in Chicago. Could it be possible that my editor didn't yet know I wasn't coming back? From what I had gathered from the Deadwood weekly, *The Pioneer*, the companies that had fought the summer campaign had just disbanded at Fort Robinson, in Nebraska. Maybe I had been reported missing in action against the Sioux, and was presumed a dead hero. I smiled at the thought. A hero rather than a man who helped a cowardly deserter. Then a sudden thought occurred to me: Maybe I should telegraph my editor that I had resigned, and request my summer's pay. I would tell him I had decided to prospect for gold. I tried to estimate what my salary would amount to for three or four months. It should be at least four hundred dollars. That would sure help offset the damnably expensive stage fare and the cost of the basic staples in the Hills. I resolved to give it a try when we reached Cheyenne. I had nothing to lose except the cost of a telegram.

About twelve-thirty we reached the first stage station, a log affair with a barn and a small corral, about ten to twelve miles from Deadwood. We all alighted to stretch our legs while the teams were being changed by the station keeper and stock handler. With the story of the robbery at this station still fresh in my mind, I paced around with my hand on the walnut butt of my Colt under my corduroy coat. I didn't go near the log station, but just stepped behind a tree at the edge of the woods to relieve myself.

The teams were changed quickly and without incident as I looked around at the silent wilderness of wooded hills that closed in on every side of the clearing. In about fifteen minutes we were on our way again.

It must have been almost an hour later when what I

was secretly dreading finally happened. The gentle rocking of the stage was lulling me into a doze, in spite of the chilly breeze puffing in the right-side window where I was sitting. The horses had slowed to a walk on a long upgrade when the coach suddenly lurched to a stop.

I snapped fully awake, thinking we had jammed a wheel against a boulder. But just as my eyes focused, I found myself staring into the open end of a double-barreled shotgun pointing in the window on my side.

"Everybody out!" came the abrupt command. Even though I had halfway expected a holdup, I'm sure my face reflected my surprise at the suddenness of it. "Move!" the voice snapped when we were slow to obey his first command. The masked robber backed his horse as I swung the door open and stepped stiffly out, followed by the other five passengers. The road was narrow at this point, dropping off a few feet to the right into a steep, pine-covered hillside.

The mounted robber wore a sugar sack over his head, with only two holes cut for his eyes. He wore a hat over this. He held his horse with his left hand, and the short, double-barreled shotgun never wavered in his right.

We lined up alongside the coach, with our hands in the air. Glancing slightly to my left, I could see another masked rider holding a Winchester on the guard and driver. The driver had his right foot on the brake and still held the reins in one hand over his head. Sheriff Pierce's shotgun was nowhere in sight. Apparently, he had been caught as much by surprise as those of us inside.

"Okay, everyone put all your valuables on the ground in front of you. Turn your pockets inside out."

We reluctantly complied.

"Just got this damned watch fixed," Curt muttered to me as he leaned down to put it on the ground.

"Quiet!" the masked man commanded.

When we had finished, the robber hooked his shotgun over his saddle horn by a leather thong and dismounted. He slipped off his saddlebags and quickly began scooping up the change, the watches and wallets on the ground, as his companion held his rifle on all of us. When he had finished, he quickly searched the men, and flipped Cathy's jacket open, but didn't touch her. Our gold was still safe. Then he went to the rear luggage boot and I could hear him rummaging around.

"Throw down the box!" the other man ordered the sheriff while this was going on. Grunting and heaving, Sheriff Pierce finally struggled over past the driver and dropped the heavy green box. The iron-bound wooden box landed with a thump and didn't bounce.

As all this was going on, I had somewhat recovered from my first fright and was able to begin looking more closely at the two highwaymen, trying to determine if there was anything distinctive about them. Both men's horses were sorrels, with no distinguishing marks. Their brands had been obliterated. Their gear consisted of well-worn Texas saddles and unadorned bridles. The man with the Winchester wore a black hat over his sack mask and an old, blue Army coat that was frayed and patched. It could have been left over from the war. The man who was ransacking the rear boot came back into my line of sight. Over a pair of overalls he wore a dirty suit coat and had a blue bandanna tied around his neck.

Ratty as they looked, they seemed to know exactly what they were doing. They were quietly efficient and coordinated, without a trace of nervousness.

"Back in the coach!" came the order from the bandit nearest us. I know fewer than five minutes had elapsed since we had first been stopped.

We obediently climbed back inside and automatically sought the same seats we had vacated.

"Move it out, driver, and don't look back!" I heard the deep command, muffled by the sugar-sack mask.

Immediately, the whip cracked and the coach lurched into motion again, the horses straining to haul us up the hill. We had covered about fifty yards, and the coach began to level off and pick up speed on the crest when I stuck my head out the window and looked back. The two, one mounted and one afoot, stood motionless, watching us out of sight. The express box still lay on the ground at their feet. Then we rounded a curve and started down the grade, and the robbers were lost to view. Almost immediately, we heard two shots.

"Shootin' the lock off," Curt remarked.

"Too heavy to carry off as is, I guess."

For the first time, the well-dressed stranger opposite me spoke. "They'll be in for a surprise when they open it." A tight, humorless grin stretched the heavy mustache.

"How's that?" Curt asked.

"Besides some rocks, they're going to find a very irritated rattlesnake."

Curt, Cathy, and I exchanged surprised glances.

"How do you know?" I finally asked.

"Because I helped put it there."

"What?"

"Of course. I'm a banker. I have money and gold going out on these stages just like a lot of other people. It's in my best interests to help discourage these robbers. I cooked up this idea with Agent Bundy."

"This was a decoy, then?"

"Right."

"When is the real gold going out?"

"I don't know. And I don't want to know. I imagine the Wells Fargo agent is one of the few people who has that information, since it's his responsibility."

He stretched his mouth in that thin, humorless grin and sat back, hooking his thumbs in his vest pockets. As he pulled his coat back, I caught the glimmer of a gold watch chain. It only slowly penetrated my consciousness. But then it struck me, and for a few seconds I heard nothing more of the conversation. All the men had been personally searched, but this man still had his watch? The banker noticed my stare, and suddenly pulled his coat closed and buttoned it. I still couldn't reconcile what I had seen. I tried to remember if the robber had been in a hurry or nervous. But I couldn't remember. I had been so preoccupied myself, hoping our own gold wouldn't be discovered, and uneasy that the robbers would get edgy and start shooting, that I had not paid enough attention as we were being searched. I started to ask him, but some instinct held me silent.

I glanced at Curt, but if he had noticed the same thing, he gave no indication. And neither did Cathy, who sat between us.

". . . Jacob Stoudt is the name," the banker was saying, extending his hand to Curt, his smile widening. "That's spelled S-t-o-u-d-t."

"Curt Wilder," Curt replied, taking the outstretched hand. "And these are my friends, Cathy Jenkins, Wiley Jenkins, and Matt Tierney."

Stoudt touched his hat to Cathy as he acknowledged the introductions. It seemed odd to me that this man who had not spoken a word to us until after the robbery, was now so friendly and expansive. It was as if a weight had been lifted from him. He no longer seemed nervous. But maybe, since he had been in on setting up the surprise, he had just been uneasy, halfway expecting we would be robbed. Sometimes shared misfortune makes friends of strangers. Surely there could be no other explanation.

Our coach pitched rhythmically as the horses picked up the pace on the level. The driver didn't stop until we hit the next station at Little Meadow.

"Everybody okay in there?" he inquired, opening the door for us as the team was being unhitched.

"You're mighty concerned about us if you're just now askin'," Wiley remarked sourly as we stepped out.

"Well, I could see weren't nobody shot," the driver replied evenly, "so I figured to get the hell outta there before somebody was."

Through the entire episode, and through our ride so far, the bearded miner had not said a word, as if being held up were all in a day's work. But I also noticed that his pockets had contained only a jackknife, a few small coins, and a plug of tobacco. Either his money was well hidden, had been in his luggage, or he knew better than to travel with money. Maybe he had wired it ahead.

The robbery, so quick and sure, was only an hour or so behind us, yet it already seemed almost like a dream. During the stop, we checked our luggage, and the driver checked his packages. Nothing appeared to be missing.

"Except for a few dollars and a few personal items, those two had mighty lean pickings today," the banker chuckled, patting his leather valise back into its place. "Unless you count a little snake venom as a surprise bonus."

The teams were changed and we went on, not stopping for supper until dark. It was at a low log station somewhere in the western Hills. Even though Wiley had brought some food, we chanced the fare in the stage station. The stew was thin and watery, and the beef or venison in it was tough and full of gristle. It was served up by a villainous-looking station keeper who apparently hadn't bothered to bathe in several months. I could hardly wait to get back outside to some fresh air.

After we were bouncing and sliding along again over the winding road, Wiley took out his knife and carved us some cheese and bread from the canvas pack he had brought inside with him. We shared with the banker and the miner.

As the night hours wore slowly on, all of us, one and two at a time, began to nod. Packed together as we were, the jouncing of the coach threw us against each other. It was as black as velvet inside the coach, since we had untied and let the leather window curtains unroll to keep out the cold wind.

I dozed, was bounced awake, and dozed again. Sometime in the small hours of early morning I was vaguely conscious of voices outside and lantern light coming and going. But I couldn't bring myself awake, and really didn't want to, since the coach had stopped rocking.

I came fully awake sometime in the predawn blackness. It must have been about four o'clock. My neck was stiff, and my feet cold and swollen. I had a terrible taste in my mouth. The miner was snoring in a far corner, from what I could hear. I pulled aside the leather curtain beside me and looked out. But the darkness was absolute. Beyond the light thrown by the lantern attached to that side of the coach, I could see nothing. The rattling of chains and squeaking of harness mingled with the thudding of the trotting horses' hooves. I dropped the curtain and tried to wedge myself into the corner of the smooth leather seat for a nap. My gritty eyeballs told me I needed it.

When I was again jolted awake by an extra hard bounce, it was full daylight. Sometime during the night we had dropped down out of the Hills to the west and were now heading almost due south across the gently rolling plains of Wyoming toward Cheyenne. At a breakfast stop a short time later I discovered we had changed drivers, and our team now consisted of four horses instead of six.

The sun and a moderate south wind had melted most of the snow and nearly dried the road. Remaining patches of snow in the sheltered hummocks were the only reminder that winter had only retreated and was lying in wait. The driver, apparently aware of this, was really moving the team, and we had to brace ourselves as the high Concord coach bounced and pitched over the dun-colored prairie. We made good time all day, stopping several more times to change teams. After a half-hour supper stop at sundown, our mud-spattered coach went rolling into the next night, with another fresh man at the reins.

The next day we left the stage stops stretched out behind us one after another like knots in a long string: Eagles Nest, Chugwater, Bear Springs, Pole Creek. Late in the afternoon I stuck my head out the window at a shout from the box. And there was Cheyenne, several miles ahead.

It was nearly suppertime when our coach finally wheeled to a stop in front of the Wells Fargo station. Sheriff Pierce was still riding shotgun, even though there was nothing more to guard—unless the whole robbery was a ruse and we were actually carrying treasure somewhere aboard.

We all climbed out stiffly and retrieved our luggage from the rear boot. I was slightly numb from the trip, both physically and mentally, even though we had made Cheyenne in good time.

The banker and the miner both disappeared on business of their own, and the four of us headed for the nearest hotel. We had grown so used to the high prices of Deadwood that our rooms seemed almost cheap by comparison.

Next morning, when we had a chance to look around, we could see that Cheyenne was also in the midst of a boom. Buildings were going up everywhere, and the growing city was swarming with people. The railroad and the Army were mainly responsible for the boom; it hardly resembled the Cheyenne we remembered from the previous May.

It was the presence of the army in town that caused us to keep our hats pulled low over our faces when outside our rooms. And we three men hadn't shaved in several days. But nobody looked twice at us.

The train was due in at 10 A.M., and we were at the depot in time to see the glistening black locomotive come puffing and wheezing in from California.

As we sat warming ourselves over coffee, I could see the distress of imminent parting in Curt's eyes. We had divided up our gold dust and converted it to greenbacks. There was nothing left to do except to say good-bye, but we were all strangely tongue-tied. When the conductor finally called, "Boooorrd!" we went silently out onto the platform, and I gave Cathy a hug and gripped Wiley's hand. "We'll look for you in the spring, then?"

He smiled wanly. "If I'm still around, I plan to be back. Nothing is for sure, though."

"Hell, things will look better when you're well and it's warm and sunny and you have a good meal under your belt. We'll stash your share of the gold we find. You'll have a good, fat poke when you get back, and you won't even have to work for it," I grinned, shaking him gently by the shoulder. I was surprised at how thin he felt even through his coat.

" 'Boooorrd!" the conductor yelled again. A gust of cold wind swirled the smell of acrid coal smoke down from the stack of the engine that was panting and steaming nearby. I glanced over my shoulder and glimpsed Cathy and Curt locked in an embrace in the crowd.

The whistle shrilled, and we rushed Wiley and Cathy onto the steps of their coach and handed up their packs just before the train began to move. The crowd surged forward in a sea of faces and waving arms as the coach windows slid past. There was an emptiness in the pit of my stomach as I watched their train roll away and shrink into the distance, a stream of gray smoke blowing straight out to the south. Both of us continued to stand looking while the crowd dispersed around us, until the caboose was only a speck on the plains.

"C'mon, Curt, she'll be back. Let's go send a telegram to the *Times-Herald*. They owe me a summer's pay. And I sure as hell earned it."

CHAPTER 11

"Raise you two."

"See your two and call." There was the muted click of ivory chips being tossed onto the green felt.

"Pair o' nines."

"Three jacks." Chuck Bundy smiled and raked in the small pile of chips.

"Deal me out," Curt said, tossing in his cards and shoving away from the table. "At the rate I'm going, my stake'll be cleaned out before spring." He got up and walked to the front window of the Golden Eagle Saloon, and stared out at the swirling snow.

"Think I'll quit for a while, too," I said, getting up and leaving Bundy and Sheriff Pierce to continue by themselves. I signaled Burnett behind the bar to draw me a beer, paid him, and took the mug to join Wilder at the window. The cold, pale light made our skin look strangely white compared to the yellow light of the coal-oil ceiling lamps deeper in the room.

"Looks like this one is gonna bury us," I commented, also looking out at the white stuff that was drifting up onto the boardwalk.

"Yeh. I'll bet this has shut down that new stamp mill at the Alpha and Omega Mines. They just got started the week after Christmas."

"This weather has shut down most everything." I glanced sideways at Curt. "Don't look so depressed. Just make up your mind that we're going to be here for a while." I shrugged. "After all, there's nothing we can do about it even if we wanted to."

109

"I guess you're right. But this is only mid-January, and we haven't seen the ground in at least six weeks."

"I know. I'm getting cabin fever, too. At least I've got a deadline every week to get something written for the paper."

"How do you find anything to report on when everyone left in town is living like a mole?"

I grinned. "There may not be much going on outside, but you forget that I used to be both a society and a political reporter in Chicago. You have to ferret out the news. That's what I use that kid, K.J., for. He keeps me up on all these tidbits of gossip. That kid really has his ears open. This job may not pay much, but it keeps me hopping trying to get enough to fill up my columns."

"What in the world do you find to write about?"

"You've read some of my stuff. A lot of rumors about what's happening on the outside, the Indian movements, troop movements, holed-up prospectors shooting each other over some trifle, the suicide of a prostitute, speculation about when the creeks will open up in the spring, and how many more people will come in. When I'm absolutely stumped for a subject, I usually just make up an editorial and give my biased opinion on anything that comes to mind."

"One of your blasts almost got your editor into a fight with his rival."

"Well, anything for a little excitement."

"You may have excitement enough if this food shortage materializes."

"Wish you wouldn't bring up subjects like that," I answered. "I've already taken up one notch in my belt."

"The sheriff was telling me the storekeepers estimate there is only enough food, at the present rate of consumption, to last until late February, and it looks like this storm is going to delay that hunting party that was being talked up last week."

"Guess we'll just have to drink more and eat less. There's no shortage of this." I took a deep draft of my beer to follow my own advice and wiped my newly grown beard with the sleeve of my jacket.

We fell quiet and continued to stare out at the silent, drifting snow. The only sound was the monotone of the dealer and the whirring and rattling of the roulette wheel in the back of the room. About two dozen men were in the Golden Eagle, killing the long winter hours gambling with smaller or larger stakes, according to their means. It was early afternoon, but the gloom of the winter day lay on the deep room that had no side windows.

After Wiley and Cathy had left in November, we had come back to Deadwood on one of the last stages that ran into the Hills and continued to work our claim in Thunder Valley for about two weeks until the snow and the cold forced us to quit for the winter. We moved into town in December and occupied our old room at the Merchants Hotel at a cheaper rate; the hotel manager was glad to get the business. The room had had a pot-bellied stove installed that knocked off enough of the chill to make it more livable than our tent in Thunder Valley. Our hotel stove was about as effective as the stove that was just now glowing almost white-hot at the side of the room behind me. Yet I couldn't feel its warmth where we stood by the front window.

Christmas and New Year had come and gone with the gold camp's usual excessive celebration. I had taken a job as a reporter for the weekly *Pioneer*, mainly to have something to do, but Curt found time hanging heavy on his hands for the first time in his life. Even in winter garrison with the army he had had his daily routine of military drills and duties to fill the time. But now he was like a caged lion. Cathy was gone, and the only women we saw in town were married or prostitutes. As he had just proven, he was no gambler; cards and dice and roulette held little appeal for him. As long as I'd known him, he struck me as one who read little, even if there had been something to read to pass the time. He was a man of action, and in this regard he did seem out of place in this winterbound town.

"You know, I'm getting kind of tired of playing cards with Bundy and Pierce, too," I said in a low voice. "Bundy's about as short of something to do as we are since Wells Fargo got snowed out and the telegraph wires went down. And that sheriff . . . well, I don't know about him. I think the man is honest enough, but I get the impression he's a little short on brains. All he seems to think about is eating, drinking, and sex. I don't believe he's made any effort to find out who was responsible for all those stage robberies since the stages stopped running. Maybe he thinks everybody has forgotten about them. He just spends his time playing cards and breaking up fights."

"What does Bundy think about the robberies? Has he got any ideas?"

"He didn't say much at first, but I've gotten to know him fairly well since we've been playing poker. He's finally loosened up and told me that he thinks it's the work of one very well organized gang of no more than six or eight men. And he believes they are spending the winter in the Hills."

"Here in Deadwood?"

"Not necessarily, but he believes they're in the settlements, walking around among the citizens unrecognized."

"Hmmm. He must have some reasons for his theories."

"Could be just a hunch or a guess like everybody else's."

"I still think there's something fishy about that banker, Stoudt. That business of not getting his watch stolen on the stage to Cheyenne—that's the only real reason I have. But he still strikes me as suspicious. He actually acted as though he was waiting for someone to show up that day. He was even nervous before we started, as if he was afraid we were going to get a late start. And he never spoke a word to us until after the holdup. He just seemed to relax after that."

"That's no proof. Besides, he said there was a rattlesnake in that box—not treasure."

"That's what he contended. But I plied Bundy with a few drinks last week and was asking him about that. He laughed when I told him what Stoudt had said. He swore there was no snake in that express box. The box had very little gold, he told me. Said they sent out the real treasure that night by wagon under heavy guard. He suspects the only reason it eventually got through safely was that the wagon driver had to detour from his planned route due to a washed-out road. Bundy claims that even Stoudt thought the real treasure had been stolen."

"Really?"

I had finally piqued his curiosity, and he turned toward me. "Why would he claim there was a snake in the box, then?"

"Beats me. If he's the inside tip-off man for this gang, maybe he really thought his men had gotten the real gold in that holdup and just gave us that wild story to throw suspicion off himself. After all, I know he saw me looking at his watch after we got back into the coach."

"Interesting theory. I guess no one has seen the faces of any of the holdup men?"

"Not according to Bundy and the sheriff. They all wore hoods. No one has even recognized any of the horses they rode. They're apparently well-organized and very careful."

"Do you think Bundy or Sheriff Pierce could be in on it?"

"Bundy would sure be in the perfect position to have all the inside information, but he strikes me as an honest company man all the way. I think he's just out of his element here. Doesn't know how to cope with this. As for Pierce, I don't think he has either the brains or the ambition to plan or coordinate anything like this. He could be an intermediary, though—possibly give the posse wrong tips, or drag his feet just at the right time—things like that. Then he couldn't be accused of being anything but inept."

"Yeh. Things change so fast in these boom towns that Pierce might just be looking to make his pile any way he can and then get out, like most everyone else. But I guess it's not really any concern of ours. We haven't lost anything to those robbers."

"Nothing of any great value so far," I agreed, "but it sure as hell makes me mad that they got my gold watch. That Waltham was willed to me by my father, and it meant a lot to me. His name was engraved inside the back case."

"I guess we'll have to be hauling our own gold out in the spring if they still haven't put a stop to the holdups."

"Looks like it's every man for himself. I keep forgetting we're on the edge of civilization. If it's not the Indians, it's your own kind trying to do you in."

I heard a thumping on the boardwalk outside, and then the door opened and K.J. bounced in in a swirl of snow and cold air. He was all bundled up in cast-off clothes that were too large for him, but his cheeks were rosy under the old wool cap and there was a grin on his face as if he had been out enjoying a summer day. He was carrying a bundle of newspapers under one arm.

"Paper! Paaaper!" he yelled.

"Here ya go, K.J." I flipped him a twenty-five-cent piece, which he caught deftly.

"I've already read most of this while it was being made up, but it's good to see the finished product."

"You wrote part of it?"

"Yeah."

Several of the men in the room stopped gambling long enough to greet the boy and buy papers from him.

"What's the latest, K.J.?" Curt asked, "How's Missus Hayes?"

"Oh, she's doin' fine, I guess," he answered, looking away, the smile disappearing from his round face.

"What do you mean, you guess? Haven't you been staying with her?"

"Yeh. I am. We are. I mean, she's doin' okay, but there's several of us up there, and a few just comin' and goin', and she's—we're—kinda short on food. And she doesn't have her fruits and vegetables and stuff to eat or sell this time o' year."

"No problem," Curt said. "We'll take up a collection and get her stocked up right now."

"Thanks, but I think she's got a little money." He shrugged. "Leastways, I give her what I make, and I think most of the others do, too."

"What's wrong, then?"

"She's not said so, but I think she's tryin' to make the food last. That's what I wanted to tell you. I just came from the mayor's office, selling my papers."

"Yeah?"

"He and some men're in a meeting, and I heard 'em talkin' about how fast the food's runnin' out in town. They were talkin' about how we won't last till spring unless some men go out huntin' and get some meat. I think they're gonna ask who wants to go."

"Have to wait till the weather breaks," I commented, glancing out the window again. Everything was still a whirling white blur. I couldn't see the buildings across the street.

"Apparently, we're shorter of food than anyone thought," Curt said.

As if on cue, my stomach growled, and Curt laughed. "Just the thought of being short of grub's making you hungry."

"It's going to be tough, but there are some pretty good hunters in this camp, from what I've seen. If there are any elk or deer out there, they'll get 'em."

"I have half a mind to volunteer to go," Curt said. "I don't make any claims to being a hunter, but it beats sitting around here."

"Me, too. Besides, I don't feel right about eating off somebody else's efforts."

"Why? We do it all the time, but we reimburse them with money."

"I guess you're right. There's plenty of gold in this town, but everybody'd have a tough time digesting that if some fresh food isn't brought in."

"What do you say? Shall we go, too?"

"I hate cold weather, but I'm all for it. We'll have to get some warm gear, and you need a rifle."

"Hey, K.J." Curt motioned for the boy, who was conversing with Burnett at the bar. "Did the mayor say when they planned to go on this hunting party, or if they were going to ask for volunteers?"

"No. That was all I heard." He turned toward the door. "I gotta go and sell the rest of my papers. See ya."

We waved as he went out, slamming the door behind him. The bat-wing doors had been removed and replaced by a solid pine door for the winter.

"I don't know how any hunters could go out on horseback in this," I said to Curt.

"Probably won't use horses," he replied. "They'd just flounder. May have to go on snowshoes."

"Your cavalry unit used horses on that winter campaign last March on the Powder River."

"That's right, but there were some long distances involved and the snow wasn't as deep. And for the most part, we were on flatter land."

"My toes are getting cold just standing here near this door. Why don't we go down the street and see if we can get some good boots. I saw some sealskin overshoes last week at one of the dry-goods stores. Clerk told me they were tried out by the army and rejected as impractical for some reason."

CHAPTER 12

A rosy, frosty dawn was just breaking three days later as Curt and I and nine other men sat astride our mules in front of the Grand Central Hotel, ready to start. Thin jets of steam issued from the nostrils of the reluctant mules and from the muffled heads of the riders around me. Nobody spoke. We were all waiting for a little more daylight to show before starting out.

As expected, the mayor had asked for volunteers, and had received many more than needed, so the group was narrowed down to our eleven, most of them weathered trappers, miners, and frontiersmen. Curt and I had to exaggerate our hunting abilities to persuade Deadwood officialdom to let us go. We also told them we were well aware of the hazards. We told them that I was from snowy Chicago and Curt from Philadelphia, and that we had years of experience on the plains and in the Rockies in winter weather. All of us had snowshoes strapped to our saddles, and our saddlebags were filled with fried bacon and biscuits, some pemmican and dried fruit, and several pounds of grain for our animals. Curt had bought a used Winchester, and we were garbed in heavy overcoats, two pairs of wool pants, and hats with earflaps. Two of the old hands wore underwear of perforated buckskin under double-breasted flannel shirts. One wore a coat of buffalo, and the other a coat of bearskin.

There was a small crowd of townspeople standing on the boardwalk to see us off as the leader of our group raised his arm and silently motioned us forward. We moved south up the snowy street toward the upper end of town.

After the storm had stopped two days before, the sky had cleared and the temperature had dropped well below zero. Then a strong wind had sprung up, swirling the powder snow about fifty feet in the air and creating a ground blizzard. Even though the sky was clear, the visibility for the rest of the day was nil. Those who had to go outside fought their way from building to building, groping, their faces averted from the stinging blast. Most of us huddled around the potbellied stoves and talked of better days. But the result of all this wind was the scouring off of much of the snow that had fallen. It was redistributed. Buildings and tree lines became snow fences. Where snow had been two feet deep on the lee side of Main Street buildings, it was now twelve feet. But, on the other hand, bare ground was visible in many places and the snow was only a few inches deep in others. Iron-hard ruts were even exposed on part of Main Street. As we cleared the edge of town, I looked up at the ridge on my left. Pines that I knew to be about thirty feet tall were showing only the top six to ten feet of their green branches above the drifts. The contours of the familiar landscape were completely changed. There was only a scattering of pink clouds above as the rising sun touched the glittering white ridges. I pressed a hand against my chest to be sure I felt the lump of my dark glasses in an inside pocket. Snow blindness could be fatal out here.

The wind had abated, and the old-timers in our party had predicted the temperature would rise into the twenties today. They also predicted that the big, foraging animals that had been confined by the storm, like the elk and deer, and possibly some buffalo, would be out pawing for the dry, brown grass in the areas that had been swept almost clean of snow.

We had gone only about a half mile beyond town when our leader held up and directed us to split up and start out in different directions. He sent us in groups of two and three, and Curt and I paired off.

"If you hear any shootin', come arunnin' toward the sound, and we'll all help dress 'em and cart the meat back to town," he told us through his thick beard. "Sound'll carry a long way on a day like this, so you shouldn't have any trouble hearin' the shots," he continued. "If you get outta earshot, or don't hear nothin', we'll all meet back here about dark."

He went into no further details, since all of our party were experienced hunters who used their own techniques. But, even as Curt and I rode away from the others, I almost wished we had teamed up with a third hunter.

We started off the road to our right, following a shallow canyon, but we soon found that the snow had drifted deep into this low land, so we guided our floundering mules off to the left and up the gradual slope through some widely spaced trees where the snow was not over a foot deep. It was about a quarter mile to the top of the ridge, where we reined up to let our mules blow for a few minutes.

"That north wind must've scoured the snow off the ridge top here and dropped it in the valleys," Curt said, his voice muffled in the scarf that covered the lower half of his face. "Wind'll do some strange things." He swung his arm in an arc, and I saw the grass poking through here and there among the pine trunks.

We dismounted and led our mules—to stretch our legs and to get some circulation going in our cold toes. By silent agreement, we followed the path of least resistance along the top of the ridge, weaving in and out of the trees, ducking low-hanging limbs and detouring around those limbs that swept to the ground.

We walked about a mile or more before my fingers and toes felt warm enough to enable me to remount. Because of the effort required by walking in the heavy clothes and the need for caution, we spoke very little. But our eyes were constantly sweeping both sides of the ridge and the valleys on either side for any sign of wildlife. The only signs of life we saw were some fresh rabbit tracks that crossed our path two or three times.

After another hour we finally came to a point where we either had to retrace our steps or abandon our mules and don our snowshoes to cross an intervening valley of deep snow. The sun was high and blinding on the white world around us, and we both put on our tinted glasses. We sat down in the soft snow to rest and discuss our next move.

"What time would you say it is?" I asked, digging into my saddlebags for something to eat.

"I'd guess between eleven and noon," Curt answered. He leaned on one elbow and gnawed off a big bite of the biscuit and bacon I handed him.

"You ever walked on snowshoes before?" I asked.

"No. Have you?"

"Nope."

"I did ask one of those mountaineers for a few pointers when I found out we were going."

I tethered the mules to a small pine, scooped a few handfuls of grain from the saddlebags, dumped them into the nosebags, and slipped them over the mules' heads. Then I grabbed a biscuit and joined Curt on the soft snow in the relative warmth of the sun. We ate quietly, staring around at the beautiful white world, with the dazzling brightness of the ridges and valleys set off by the dark green spruce and pines marching up and down the blanketed hillsides. It was a picturesque, though totally silent, world. Even the birds who hadn't migrated south seemed to be in hiding. The munching of our mules sounded loud in the stillness. There was no wind where we sat, but as I glanced around I noticed that the wind must be blowing high up, because some thin clouds were sliding up over the rim of the next ridge from the west and were spreading slowly over the blue dome above.

"Now I'm thirsty," Curt said, slipping his bare hand back into his glove and pushing himself to his feet.

"We could build a fire and melt down some snow, or melt the ice in our canteens," I replied.

"Not now. Let's not waste the daylight. It's clear there's no game in sight. Shall we cut across here and take a look over the next ridge?"

"Might as well."

I took the empty nosebags off the mules and brought the snowshoes from our saddles.

When we strapped them on and took our first tentative steps, we nearly tripped ourselves. But with a little careful practice we finally got the knack of moving forward on the unwieldy webbed feet.

"I'll break trail for a while," Curt offered. "Then we'll switch."

We slung our canteens over our shoulders, our rifles across our backs, stuffed a couple more biscuits with bacon into our side pockets, and started.

After about a hundred yards, Curt halted and leaned down to tighten a rawhide lacing. We were both gasping, and we stood for a few minutes until our pounding hearts steadied down. Then I took the lead. Breaking trail involved lifting one leg, swinging the foot forward and down—where it sank several inches into the soft powder—then repeating the action with the other leg, all the while keeping the legs unnaturally wide apart to keep from stepping on one's own snowshoes.

After twenty steps my heart was pounding; after fifty steps, sweat was beginning to trickle down from under my cap. After a few hundred steps, my mouth was dry and my thigh muscles were crying for mercy. I stopped and leaned on my knees in agony, sucking in the cold air, my breath whistling in and out.

"See what town living has done to us?" I gasped to Curt, who was breathing about as hard as I was. He nodded in silent agreement, and then moved around in front of me and started off again.

Alternating, we struggled across the valley and ascended part way up the other ridge before we stopped to take off the snowshoes and suck at our half-frozen canteens. Our clothes were wet inside with perspiration.

While we sat regaining our breath and our strength, I noticed it had gotten perceptibly darker, and I took off my tinted glasses. The clouds were pouring in heavier and lower, darkening the entire sky and blotting out the sun. I saw Curt noticing it, too, as he slipped his glasses into an inside pocket.

About five minutes later Curt motioned with his head and we got to our feet and finished climbing the ridge, slipping and sliding in knee-deep snow, sometimes pulling ourselves up the steepest parts by grabbing limbs. Just before we crested the timbered ridge, we crouched and slowed. Cautiously, we raised our heads, and instantly I caught a glimpse of movement. It was a small herd of six or seven buffalo pawing and nosing the snow away to graze at the base of a small bluff below us, about two hundred yards away.

Curt put out his arm to hold me back, but I wasn't going anywhere. We both got down on all fours and edged our way forward to the base of a big pine. The snow was clinging to the shaggy humps and heads of the great beasts in the protected area at the base of the bluff, as they scuffed the shallow snow away for the brown grass underneath. Now and then, one or another of them would lift its head and sniff the air or look around, but we stayed still, and they went back to their main business of securing food.

"Look at all those steaks!" I whispered near Curt's ear. "Think they're within range?"

"Not really," he whispered back. He glanced up at the darkening sky. I rubbed my eyes; they seemed to have a smoky film over them as I looked down from under our tree into the shallow valley. Then it suddenly dawned on me that it had started to snow again. The air was filled with tiny snowflakes drifting silently down on our silent, gray-white world. Except for the Winchesters in our hands and our woven clothes, we might have been ice-age cavemen ready to strike a herd of mammoths with our flint-tipped spears.

The millions of small flakes created an indistinct haze, but they would help muffle the sounds of our moving toward the herd.

We squirmed forward, trying to keep our weapons out of the soft snow. When one of the herd lifted his head, we immediately froze. Their eyesight was not keen, and even if they noticed our creeping down the white hillside, they might mistake us for wolves, which healthy adult buffalo don't worry about.

I was certainly no expert on buffalo, or on hunting,

for that matter, so I was relying on Curt to lead the way. We plowed slowly forward down the steep slope, trying to move only when the animals weren't looking our way, but we were now out from under the protection of the trees and were highly visible, even through the falling snow.

We had managed to work our way almost to the bottom of the slope and to within a hundred yards of the buffalo when one of them jerked his head up, snorted loudly, and all of them began to move unhurriedly away from us along the base of the low bluff opposite, a big bull breaking the trail for the others in the foot-deep snow. Finally, about a quarter-mile away, they encountered deeper snow and all came to a halt and began to swing their lowered heads from side to side, burrowing down to the buried grass.

Disgustedly, I stood up, brushing the snow off. Curt and I looked at each other. "Couple of great hunters!" I said.

"I don't think we spooked them," Curt replied. "Takes a lot to really scare 'em off." He slipped off one glove, raised the earflaps of his hat, and scrubbed a hand over his face and ears, rubbing the snow from his short, dark beard and mustache. His ears, nose, and cheeks were rosy. "Probably should have taken a couple of long shots when we had the chance," he admitted.

"Want to go after them? They look like they may be stopped by that deep snow up there."

"Don't be fooled by that. They got into this valley somehow, and they'll be able to get out."

"You don't think they might have been in here when it first started snowing and trapped them?"

"Possible, I guess. I'm as new to the Hills as you are. I thought most buffalo herds migrated south on the plains as winter begins to set in."

"A few strays who waited too long, maybe."

"Could be. What say we give it one more try before heading back?"

"I'm with you."

We plowed on clumsily toward the opposite bluff in knee-deep snow, ignoring the even clumsier snowshoes that hung by rawhide thongs down our backs. My toes, fingers, and nose were again hurting from the cold. We reached the partial shelter of the fifteen-foot bluff and then turned and walked due north toward the distant herd, with no attempt at concealment. The snow had begun to fall thicker and faster now, and a fresh north wind was blowing it directly in our faces. We were approaching them from downwind, with the heavily falling snow to mask us from their weak eyes, and with the deeper drifts behind them to hinder their escape.

My eyes were watering from the stinging blast of wind-whipped snow being driven straight at us. We walked slowly and deliberately, and in this way were able to approach to within fifty yards of the herd before they apparently noticed us and began to move around nervously, as if looking for a way to escape. They were no longer attempting to graze. Mostly, they stood with their backs to the storm and their great, shaggy heads with the short, curved horns hanging low. They moved their heads from side to side to see us better. Curt motioned for me to move off to one side, away from the bluff and into deeper snow.

"Don't shoot at the head," he cautioned me in a low voice. "The bone and that matted hair are too thick. Let's take that big one in front who's turned a little away from us."

I dropped to one knee in the two-foot-deep snow, threw off my gloves, levered a round into the chamber, and brought the ice-cold wood of the stock to my cheek.

"Aim just behind the hump," Curt said, preferring to shoot from a standing position behind and just to the left of me. I heard him throwing the lever.

"Ready?"

I nodded. The buffalo still had not moved.

"On the count of three. One . . . two . . three!"

Our Winchesters roared as one. The bull buffalo at the head of the herd jerked slightly sideways, staggered several steps, and fell forward, rolling onto his side. Even then, the rest of the herd didn't panic, but did begin to move slowly away from us and plow up the gradual slope at the end of the valley.

We jumped up and struggled to our kill. One or both of us had apparently hit him in a vital spot.

"We'd better signal the others in case they didn't hear our shots," I said.

Curt immediately fired three quick rounds into the air. There was no ringing crash or echo. The soft, swirling atmosphere seemed to absorb the sound like a feather pillow.

We stood for a few seconds without speaking. I believe both of us were wondering how far the sound had carried. Even if it was heard, it would be at least an hour or two before any of the hunting party could reach us. Intent on making our kill, we had not noticed how heavy the snow had become.

"Think we ought to backtrack and meet them?" I asked. Even as the words left my mouth, I knew it was a ridiculous suggestion. What had started as a light snow had become a full-sized storm. Moreover, the wind had picked up. It was impossible to see more than a few yards in any direction. Not only could we not go back to meet them, but they would never be able to find us, at least until the storm abated. Curt didn't laugh at my suggestion. I think the gravity of the situation had suddenly hit him also. Instead, he leaned near my ear and half shouted over the wind, "We'd better find some protection to weather this storm. I don't think this is just a hard flurry. We'll have to ride it out."

"Shall we gut this buffalo before he freezes stiff?"

"No time. We have to get to shelter—fast!"

"What's the rush?"

"I've been caught in blizzards like this before on the plains. I've seen men freeze to death only a few feet from safety. Went out of camp to feed the stock. Didn't hold onto a line to find their way back and got confused."

"Where to, now?"

"If we could get back to the top of that last ridge, there are some big pines with limbs that form a tent with the ground."

"Think we can find the ridge?" A cold feeling was in the pit of my stomach. The snow was swirling thicker than ever.

"I think it's back that way, and I usually have a pretty good sense of direction. But the only way I'm sure is in relation to the way that bull pointed when he fell."

"Let's go, then."

But Curt grabbed my arm. "Hold it. We wouldn't get ten yards before we'd be completely lost."

"What do we do, then?" I tried to keep the edge of fear out of my voice. I noticed I couldn't even feel my feet, and my fingers were paining me, even though I had quickly pulled my gloves back on after shooting.

"Quick! Get your knife!"

While I was fumbling for my knife beneath my coat, he already had his out and was crouched by the belly of the dead buffalo. The wind and snow were causing my eyes to water so badly I couldn't see anything distinctly.

When I finally joined him, knife in hand, he had already slit open the belly, and blood was staining the snow.

"His body will stay warm for a while!" he shouted in my ear. "And it'll provide some protection from the wind."

I looked at him blankly, partially numbed by the bitter blast.

"Come on! Scoop out this snow and make a pit. We're on the lee side."

I followed his example, using a snowshoe as a shovel, and the effort helped drive some warmth back into my chilling shoulders and arms. The wind was cutting right through all my protective clothing.

In only two or three minutes we had a snug trench about two feet deep, and had piled the snow up another foot or two around us, with the body and legs helping to form three sides of the pit. Once we were down out of the wind, it felt almost comfortable in the soft shelter.

"Get those sealskin overshoes off and put your feet and hands inside that carcass," Curt said. "It'll keep 'em from freezin'."

"Right."

I had to use the heels of both hands to get the over-shoes off, since my fingers wouldn't grip. But I finally managed. We had left a narrow ledge of packed snow next to the body so we could take turns lying on our sides with hands and feet thrust into the slippery, visceral, abdominal cavity of the great beast. It didn't take long for the animal's warmth to penetrate right through my boots and wool socks. The sensation of returning feeling, even though painful, was the most welcome feeling I believe I had ever experienced.

After a few minutes we switched, and Curt warmed his extremities the same way.

I lost track of time. Minutes became hours, yet the leaden afternoon overcast quickly faded into night.

I thought I had experienced wind when I lived in Chicago, but I had felt nothing but a breeze compared to the howling, sub-zero blast that tore over our heads that night.

Our speech became slurred from our numbed chins, and we sounded like two drunks. We laughed at the ridiculous similarity. When we weren't trying to capture the fading heat from the dead buffalo, we were rubbing each other's hands and toes—in an effort to keep awake as much as to restore circulation. We did no violent exertions, so as to preserve the strength that was being expended rapidly enough by our bodies in fighting the cold. We dug out our remaining biscuits and bacon and ate them, then sipped some of the unfrozen water from our canteens.

The trench was big enough for us to stretch out almost full length side by side, but for what seemed like hours I resisted the temptation to lie down.

But finally, my mental processes began to break down. More than once, I came to my senses with Curt slapping my face. But I slid right back into lethargy. I was so fatigued that I wanted nothing in the world so much as a good, satisfying sleep.

"Dammit, Matt, wake up!" The stinging blast of a snow-covered glove hit my face, and instinctively I fought back. But Curt took my weak swings on his arms and shook me violently.

"Hang on, Matt! Talk to me!"

"I'm warm now, Curt," I mumbled irritably. "Let me take a little nap. Won't sleep long. Just a few minutes."

"Wake up, or you'll die! Do you hear me?" the voice shouted next to my covered ear, "You'll die!"

By a mighty effort of will I brought myself partially alert again when the shaking and the words finally penetrated. I moved around in the hole and worked my arms and legs. The storm was still roaring horizontally overhead in the blackness, and I thought, in a rational moment, that it was very ironic we had matches in our pockets, but nothing to build a fire with.

But then the deadly fatigue encircled me with its comfortable arms again and the steady roaring of the wind gradually faded into nothingness.

CHAPTER 13

It was only after I had been at Mrs. Hayes's house for three days that I fully realized how close to death I had come. Even then, I could not remember the details of the rescue; it came back to me in intermittent flashes of scenes when I recalled feeling intense pain and being carried on an improvised sled of fresh-smelling pine limbs and brilliant flashes of blinding sunlight on snow.

Curt wasn't in quite as bad shape as I was. Although he had two frostbitten toes, he was able to help the rest of the hunting party who had been searching for us. In fact, he was the one who was able to signal them with rifle shots the next morning when the storm had abated. Three or four of the others had suffered some slight frostbite when they were also caught by surprise in the blizzard.

No doctor had wintered in Deadwood, so I was taken to the charitable Mrs. Hayes's house to be cared for.

"You're damn lucky you didn't lose any toes, Matt," was Curt's greeting as he helped me out of bed the third morning and walked me around.

"He's right," Mrs. Elvira Hayes chipped in, slipping a copper teakettle onto the hot iron stove. "Lucky they got you here when they did. If I hadn't been able to soak the frost outta them toes gradual-like, they'd 'a' probly mortified and pizened your blood. You coulda died. Seen it happen b'fore. It's either cut 'em off or die," she finished succinctly, with her usual humorless expression.

Curt laughed. "Nothing like laying it on the line."

We pulled straight chairs up to her rough pine table, and she set two tin cups in front of us.

"I thought you were supposed to rub snow on frost-bite," I said, slipping one foot out of the doeskin moc-casins and examining my toes.

"Humpf!" the old lady snorted. "Shows what you know. Don't know where that idea ever got started. That don't make no sense atall. Just freezes whatever's frozen all the more. Gotta use warm water."

I watched Mrs. Hayes greasing her skillet to fry us some thin-sliced strips of venison and wondered again what manner of woman she was. She was of indeter-minate age, anywhere from fifty to sixty-five, tall and lean, wearing a sacklike dress that reached nearly to the tops of her heavy shoes. Even though she was spare, had salt-and-pepper gray hair pulled back in a severe bun, she had a whiplike hardness to her body and motions that suggested a life of hard work. Curt was of the opinion that she was from Missouri, since he didn't believe her dialect was like an Appalachian Mountains woman. How she came to be in a place like Deadwood was a mystery to everyone. But gold rushes, like floods, deposit some unrelated flotsam in strange places. During the first rush in the spring of '76, she had appeared on the scene alone and had almost immediately begun to attract at-tention with her selflessness—an unusual trait in a town founded on greed.

Just now, K.J. and I were the only two staying at her stout log house on Williams Street. It was built on a terrace above Main and connected to it by steep wooden stairs. Curt was also occupying a cot here, to help look after me until I could get on my feet again for good. Mrs. Hayes still had upwards of two dozen visitors each day. They were usually the miners, the prostitutes, the storekeepers, rather than the self-styled elite of the new town—the bankers, the city officials, and their wives.

"Sorry I can't offer you boys some eggs to go with this venison," she growled, setting our tin plates on the table, "but the chickens ain't been layin' lately." She didn't crack a smile, but I chuckled.

"Well, the least you could do, then, is give us some fried potatoes and bread to go with it," I complained in

mock seriousness, knowing full well there were no potatoes
in town and very little flour, which was being rationed
out.

She didn't reply, but only grabbed the corner of her
apron, opened the door of the stove, and raked a poker
around in the fire before slamming the door shut again.

All of us in the hunting party were the heroes of the
town, and could have anything we wanted merely for the
asking. We had literally saved the town from starvation
by bringing in one buffalo, three deer, and an elk. There
was still some food and some frozen beef left.

"You know, it's really kind of scary when I think of
how suddenly that storm hit us," I remarked to Curt as
Mrs. Hayes sat down to eat with us.

"I recognized the signs, but almost too late," he answered. "A blizzard like that can be more vicious than a
tornado. At least a twister passes quicker, and it either
gets you or it doesn't."

"Sorry I wasn't much help in hauling that meat back."

"I wasn't much help, either. The rest of the party had
gotten caught out like we did, but most of them were able
to get sheltered under trees or in windbreaks where there
was firewood. Good thing that storm passed over in a
few hours. I've known 'em to last for a couple of days
without letup."

"My memory's pretty hazy. How long did it take someone to find us?"

"Well, I couldn't rouse you, so I just kept firing my
Winchester every few minutes, and they got there about
three hours after daylight. 'Course our backtrail was wiped
out, but they found us by the sound. Our mules had
jerked loose and gone back toward town. They found 'em
on the road."

"Were you able to stay awake all night?"

"Just barely. When they got to us, I collapsed and they
had to carry me back, too."

"How long did it take? I remember fading in and out.
It seemed like forever."

"Most of the day. But they got some help when they

got us to the road. More men came out from town to help."

"They musta had a helluva time with that buffalo carcass."

"They did. Burnett went out to help bring it in, and it was frozen hard as a rock. They had to saw it up into smaller pieces to be able to drag it out over that deep snow."

"Maybe they should have waited a few days. It looks like a spring thaw is setting in out there now," I commented, glancing out the window at the brilliant sunshine and the icicles dripping from the eaves.

"Yeh, it started really warming up yesterday, and today's started out the same. Must be the Black Hills' version of the Chinook wind."

"What's that?"

"A warm west wind that blows for a few days and causes a midwinter thaw."

"Nature's way of sayin 'I'm sorry,' I guess."

"Or of letting us know that warm weather will eventually be back."

"Where's K.J. this morning?" I asked Mrs. Hayes, who had finished her meager breakfast and was picking her teeth with a broom straw as she sipped her coffee.

"Down in town, I reckon. He generally leaves early, even before I get up."

"Where did he come from, anyway?" I asked.

She shrugged. "Where do any o' them come from? Folks killed, or they left him, or he ran away. Don't rightly know. He never said and I never asked. Reckon he'll tell me if he takes a notion. It's not my place to pry into other people's affairs. Kenneth Joseph—I don't know his last name—kinda took a cotton to me." Her eyes twinkled, and she half smiled. "And I reckon the feeling was mutual. He's gonna amount to sumpin' some day, that boy."

"He'll be at a disadvantage if he doesn't get some schooling," I offered.

"He'll get enough schoolin' t'see him through," she answered, unperturbed.

"Sure wish I had some corn bread to wipe up this juice," I said, scraping my plate clean.

"That would be good," Curt said. "Too bad they're saving what corn is left to parcel out to the stock."

"Well, that was mighty good, anyway, Missus Hayes," I said, draining my coffee cup down to the grounds. "I'm feeling so good, I may take a walk to town today."

"Sure you're up to it?" Curt asked. "You may not be able to get your boots on; your feet are still swollen."

"I'll just slip on those sealskin overshoes over these moccasins you got me."

"Well, get your stuff on and I'll help you."

"Right. I've got to get out for a while. This thaw is giving me spring fever."

Thirty minutes later, Curt was helping me down the back steps that connected Williams Street to Main. We first went by my newspaper office, where the editor, Jack Colcroft, pounded my back in greeting, then quickly assigned me the job of writing up my personal account of our harrowing experience.

"This will give us a real exclusive, even on those two new dailies that are just trying to get off the ground," he told me. He was a tall, balding man, with quick, nervous movements and an easy smile.

"When's it due?" I asked.

"Just as soon as you can get it to me," he replied. "We'll put out a special edition."

"Okay, Jack." I smiled ruefully. "I wouldn't have stopped in if I had known you were going to put me to work so soon."

He slapped me on the back again as we went out. "I'll be looking for that piece by tomorrow."

I limped on down the boardwalk, breathing in the milder air and feeling the warmth of the morning sun that was finally penetrating the deep gulch. I could hear water dripping and gurgling and gushing everywhere as the snow was melted rapidly by the warm wind and sun. The slushy snow on Main Street was rapidly turning into mud under wheels and hooves. The streets were alive with people—people I hadn't seen in weeks. They were walking up and down the boardwalks with no apparent purposes in mind. It was as if everyone were shaking off the lethargy of winter hibernation and coming out for a breath of fresh air.

We passed the Wells Fargo and the telegraph offices. Both were still closed. Evidently, the line to the outside world was still down. No wonder my narrow escape from freezing was still the biggest news. The rest of the world could have disappeared for all we knew.

"Hey, K.J.!"

I looked up from my reverie at Curt's call. The boy was coming down the sidewalk toward us, his old coat flopping open and his hands thrust into his side pockets. He stopped, and I could see the stoppered neck of a bottle protruding from his outside pocket.

"You're not taking up drinking, are you?" I joshed him, indicating the bottle. "At least, not before noon."

"Naw." He grinned. "This is a bottle of that medicine."

"That what? You mean elixir? From the medicine man?"

"Yeah. He gave me some for Missus Hayes."

"What's wrong with her?"

"Nothin'. It's just supposed to keep her healthy."

"Missus Hayes impresses me as the type who would concoct her own tonic if she needed one," Curt remarked to me.

"Where'd you see the medicine man?" I asked K.J. "I thought he'd left town."

"Down at the Alhambra. That's where he hangs out, mostly. Mister Mortimer's a good tipper; I run a lot of errands for him."

"What kinds of errands?"

"Oh, just different stuff. Some of it's kinda strange."

"How so?"

"It's not the usual stuff like shinin' his boots, or helpin' him hitch and unhitch that nice horse of his, or fetchin' grub to his room, or gettin' his washin' back from them Chinese. He has me do stuff like gettin' a close look at somebody's spurs, or sidlin' up to some men at the bar and listenin' to what they're talkin' about, or somethin' like that. The other day he bought one o' my papers and told me to take it up to one of the rooms and tell the man inside that it was from the hotel manager. What he really wanted me to do was see if I could get a look at the man with his shirt off or his arms bare, to see if he had a knife scar way up here on his arm."

Curt and I exchanged curious glances.

"It's fun and kinda mysteriouslike. Mister Mortimer told me he was a spy during the war and he wanted to train me to be one, too."

"He didn't tell you why he wanted to find out all these things?"

"Nope. He just told me he was real curious about a lot of things, and gave me a big tip, so I just quit askin' questions."

"I wonder if he's still selling his elixir?"

"I seen him sellin' a bottle now and then, usually down at the Alhambra at night. Some o' those miners get drunk on it," K.J. replied. "Or at least, they sure act drunk after they drink a whole bottle of it." He made a face. "It smells terrible. I took a sniff o' this bottle. Thought I might try a sip, but it smells like pine tar. Whew!"

"Is Mortimer at the Alhambra now?"

"He was. I gotta go. In this muddy weather, they's gonna be some boots need cleanin', and I wanta get to 'em first before I go to dinner at the Grand Central."

"You're eating at the Grand Central?" I asked. "That's pretty high class."

"Oh, I'm not eating in the dining room. The cook always saves the best scraps for me and hands 'em out the back door. People sure waste a lot o' good food. Besides," he said matter-of-factly, "it saves Missus Hayes's having to feed me. She has a hard enough time."

He waved, and was off up the boardwalk.

"Good kid."

"Yeah."

"Wonder who this Mortimer is? Seems like he's got more than peddlin' snake oil on his mind."

"It sure does. Might make a good story for the paper if I can get next to him and find out what he's up to."

"Always the reporter. Want to see if we can look him up right now?"

"Not just now. My feet are beginning to hurt again. How about helping me back up to Missus Hayes's place. I think maybe tomorrow I can move back up to our room, though."

As we came around the corner of a building to the stairs leading up to Williams Street, we saw Mrs. Hayes about halfway up, carrying her usual daily bucket of beer from a nearby saloon. Two well-dressed women were just crossing the open space between the buildings, holding their skirts out of the slush, and saw Mrs. Hayes at the same time.

"Mercy! Look at that old lady, sneaking around the back doors of these saloons and guzzling beer. Mighty poor example for those youngsters she keeps, if you ask me," one of them remarked to the other. "And I hear she even smokes a cob pipe, too!"

"What can you expect from somebody who welcomes harlots into her house?" the other woman replied in a lower voice as the two of them walked on out of earshot, still talking.

Curt and I looked at each other and grinned.

"What do you reckon Wiley Jenkins would have said about that?" Curt asked.

"I'd hate to think," I replied. "But I'll bet it would've scorched the bustles off those self-righteous biddies."

CHAPTER 14

The next day we moved back to our hotel room. My feet and fingers were improving rapidly. The swelling had gone down, but the itching of the dead, flaking skin was intolerable. I stayed in all day, since I couldn't stand to have moccasins or boots on.

Before cold temperatures set in again the day after, most of the snow had melted. When the mushy bare ground froze, it made Main Street rough but passable again. By the end of that week I was back to normal, and Curt and I immediately went to make the acquaintance of Mr. Floyd Mortimer, the snake-oil drummer. But he was nowhere to be found. The elixir salesman had mysteriously vanished from his old haunts at the Alhambra, and even K.J. swore he had not seen him in several days. Some discreet questions revealed that he was still registered at the Grand Central, but the desk clerk had no idea where he had gone.

To fill the time, in addition to some of my newspaper's columns, we decided then to look up Mr. Jacob Stoudt, our former stage passenger and bank executive. I had no clear idea of what I was going to ask Mr. Stoudt if and when I got an interview with him, but I thought maybe my role as a reporter would at least allow me access to him.

"You could always make up some story about wanting to interview him about life as a bank president in a frontier gold camp as compared with life as a banker back East, or wherever."

It was a pretty flimsy excuse for an interview, but I thought I'd give it a try anyway. His reaction to the stage

137

robberies would have been a meatier interview, if I hadn't suspected him of having something to do with them and wanted to avoid the subject for the time being.

But the whole thing became moot when I couldn't even find Jacob Stoudt to interview. At the second bank where I inquired, I was told by a teller that Mr. Stoudt was indeed the president, but that he seldom visited his office there, especially now during the slack business of the winter months. I was directed to his house on Main Street about a block from the bank, but a servant answered the door and told me that Mr. Stoudt was not seeing anyone without an appointment. The fact that I identified myself as a reporter mattered not at all. I would have to make an appointment through his secretary at the bank during regular business hours. Besides, the servant told me, Mr. Stoudt was out of town just now. Then I tried another tack and told the servant that I had been a passenger to Cheyenne with Stoudt when the stage had been robbed in the fall, and I wanted to interview him concerning any losses his bank had sustained since the robberies started. The black-suited young servant again told me his boss was out of town, and when I insisted on trying to make an appointment through him, he suggested I leave before he called the sheriff.

"Well, that was a waste of time," I observed to Curt as we walked back up the street.

"Not necessarily. You learned a few things. First of all, you know that Stoudt is a secretive man. Second, you know he doesn't want to see anyone he hasn't invited, including you. You know he's not too far from here, since the roads out of the hills are still covered with ice and mud. He couldn't have made it on horseback as far as Custer, sixty miles south, unless he walked and camped out along the way. Somehow, he didn't strike me as the type for that."

"So, that leaves me totally frustrated. The two men I most wanted to talk to—Mortimer and Stoudt—have both disappeared somewhere here in town."

"It does seem strange," Curt admitted. "Maybe they

know you're a reporter and for some reason don't want to talk to you."

"Well, I don't really care. Whatever's going on, I guess it's really none of our business. If it's illegal, it may be the town's business, but not ours personally. I really took this job as a reporter to have something to do during the winter, but I'm getting sick of everything now. Cabin fever has about got me. I'm ready to get back out on our claim."

"Won't be long now. Next week is March first."

"Spring can't get here too soon to suit me."

But spring did seem to be somewhere forever in the future. I dragged around town for the next two weeks, trying to get enough news, or make up enough news, to help fill the two issues of the paper that came off the Washington press under Jack Colcroft's hand. I saw nothing of either Floyd Mortimer or Jacob Stoudt. They had either vanished from Deadwood or were both in hiding.

We had one more snowfall in mid-March—about a four-incher. But it was winter's last fling. The weather rapidly moderated after that. And with the sunshine and the lengthening days came the melting of the snow, which turned the creeks into torrents and the gulch into a sea of mud.

As soon as the roads became passable again, the telegraph line was repaired, and suddenly Deadwood was part of the larger world once more. Some soldiers came and went. They were members of a detachment under a Major Brown, who had been sent up from Fort Robinson, Nebraska the previous October to winter in and around Custer and to patrol the Hills, helping to protect settlers from any roving war parties. Curt didn't recognize any of them, but he stayed out of sight when they were in town, just to be safe.

With the thaw came something else the winter residents had long been expecting and bracing for—the spring influx of gold-seekers. Earlier than I thought it possible, even before the stages began to run again, the gold-hunters began to trickle into town. By the first of April the trickle had become a flood. They came on horseback, on muleback, in wagons and every conceivable kind of rig. Some later arrivals even came by foot. Fortunately, most of the early arrivals brought their own provisions, something Deadwood was woefully short of. By mingling with these new prospectors in the saloons and restaurants, we heard of the privations and troubles some of them had already endured just getting here. Some of the more un-organized groups had suffered losses of many mules to mud fever. I had never heard of such a thing, but Curt explained that the long hair along the belly and the hair from hock to fetlock becomes so caked with mud that the pores are clogged and the mules can't sweat, causing them to die from overheating. Curt said he guessed a lot of these greenhorns were either too tired, too ignorant, or too lazy to clean off their wagon-pulling mules after a long, tiring day on the trail.

The influx of new people and the fairing weather had stirred my desire to get back out on our own claim in Thunder Valley. The feverish pace at which the new-comers were heading into the surrounding hills somehow made me feel that all the gold would be gone, and every inch of ground staked. And the continuing stream of in-coming wagons made me think there were almost enough people to do just that.

Gold fever and spring fever had gripped me so hard that I gave my editor my notice that I was quitting. He begged me to stay on, saying my chances of striking it rich were slim.

"We've got a pretty fair-looking claim, Jack," I told him. "And I'm itching to get at it."

He walked outside in his leather apron, wiping the ink from his hands on a rag.

"Why don't you take the stage down to Cheyenne?" he suggested, blinking in the bright sunlight. "I'll pay your way. From the looks of some old newspapers these new-comers have brought in with them, and what's coming in over the wire, you could gather enough news in two days to make this sheet into a daily for a few weeks— maybe permanently."

"Thanks, Jack, but I came here to find gold, and I've done only fair so far. Besides, these people who are just coming in know what's going on in the outside world. They want news of Deadwood and the Hills, and the new strikes and the stage robberies and all that."

"You may be right. I guess I can get enough national news by telegraph or from these old newspapers to fill out the columns and give the pages some variety. Let's leave it this way: If things don't work out, or if you want a little part-time work, your job's always open. I hate to lose a good, experienced reporter. Besides, the way this town's booming, I could keep three reporters busy."

I grinned and gripped his hand. "Done."

"By the way, here's a copy of *The Rocky Mountain News* I just gleaned a few items from. Thought you might want something new to read for a change."

"Thanks."

"I said 'new,' but it's hardly current. That thing's about four months old."

"Beats reading my own stuff or labels on cans."

My last remaining job was to get a story about the resumption of stage service and gold shipments, so I went to the Wells Fargo office to see Bundy. Since the stages started running, two weeks before, I had seen little of Bundy, who had been kept busy nearly fifteen hours a day in his office. There had been no reports of any holdups so far. I didn't know if this meant there had been no gold shipped and I doubted—even considering my friendship with Bundy—that I was about to find out.

"Nope, no gold shipments have gone out yet this season," Bundy told me with unexpected candor, leaning on the counter. A stage bound for Pierre had just pulled out, leaving him with a few minutes of slack time.

"Is that really the straight of it, Chuck? You wouldn't want to give me a statement for the paper, would you?"

"I don't mind. What do you want to know?"

"Can you tell me what precautions have been taken to protect the gold shipments to Cheyenne this season?"

"The company and I and Sheriff Pierce are working on some ideas we hope will work."

"Like what?"

"You know I can't tell you that for publication, Matt."
He shrugged. "Although I can't say it would make much
difference. Somehow, those robbers found out nearly every
move we made last year."

"Well, you haven't had any holdups so far this year."

"I guess they're not interested in passenger valuables,
even though all of those inbound stages from Cheyenne
and Sidney have been loaded—people hanging off them
everywhere. Probably laying back and waiting for our first
bullion shipment."

"When will that be?"

Bundy shrugged again. "We've only got a trickle of
dust so far. Hope that's not an indication of a lack of
trust in Wells Fargo. But it's early yet."

We talked on for a few more minutes until a customer
interrupted us, and I stopped jotting down notes and left,
knowing I wasn't going to get anything concrete.

As I stepped out into the sunshine of the beautiful
April day, a warm south wind was blowing along the
street, drying the mud. Curt was coming up the sidewalk.
He had been to the livery stable, checking on our animals
and settling up our bill.

"Get anything from Bundy?" he asked.

"Not much. But I don't blame him. He's really on the
spot. I wouldn't say anything at all if I were in his
position."

"How about a beer? On me."

"Sounds good. It's about lunchtime, anyway. I'm
starved for some vegetables."

"Let's try the Grand Central, then. I know their dining
room is already serving some of the tinned vegetables
that came in on that first bull train from Pierre."

"Matt! Curt!"

We heard running feet on the boards behind us and
turned to see K.J. chasing us, waving a piece of paper.

"What's up, kid?" He had shed several layers of his
floppy clothes, but what remained still engulfed his small
body.

"Telegram came for you just after you left the office."

I took the folded sheet and handed it to Curt as I reached for some coins to tip K.J.

"It's from Cathy and Wiley. They're coming back!"

"Great! When?"

"As soon as they can get a stage up from Cheyenne."

"Should be just a matter of a few days, then. I'm glad we hadn't started for Thunder Valley. We can wait for them."

"Why don't I go out to our camp and get it in shape before they get here?" Curt suggested.

"Better yet, I'll go," I said. "You stay here and meet them. I know you're anxious to see Cathy, although," I added, glancing him up and down, "she may not even recognize you."

"Why?"

"You're about as scruffy-looking a character as I've seen in these hills. Hair and beard haven't been trimmed in weeks, boots caked in mud, clothes that look like you slept in them for a week . . ."

He grinned. "You don't look as though you just stepped out of a bandbox yourself."

"I don't have a girl who's interested in me coming to town. But, come to think of it, now that warm weather seems to be here for good, I may get a bath this afternoon and send these clothes down to one of those Oriental wash houses."

"Good idea. But right now, let's get some lunch. I'm starved."

"Hey, K.J., come and join us for lunch. I'm buying," I yelled at the boy as he jumped down onto one of the planks laid out to help cross the muddy street. His dark eyes lit up with pleasure.

"Sure will." He hopped back up onto the boardwalk. "Thanks. I got some chores to do, but they can wait."

The three of us clumped on down toward the Grand Central, weaving our way through the crowd on the sidewalk. I had left my hat in our room, and the warm sun felt good through my corduroy jacket whenever we came to a break in the boardwalk roof. In spite of the mix of mud and manure in the street, the air had a soft, sweet smell of fresh pine and new flowers and earth. I took a deep breath and exhaled. It was a good day to be alive.

"Oh, no!" Curt halted abruptly, and swung toward the street, almost knocking me and K.J. into the front of the building we were passing.

"What's wrong?" I caught him by the shoulders and tried to look into his face, but he was staring at something that was passing down the street.

"I don't believe it," he breathed.

"Believe *what*?" Over his shoulder I tried to pick out what he was looking at, but the street was full of wagons, carriages, and riders, passing up and down in both directions.

"It's him again." His voice was grim but he had a look in his eyes that told me he had not even heard my questions. K.J. and I looked at each other blankly and then back at Curt.

"For God's sake, Curt! What the hell spooked you?"

"As sure as I'm standing here, that black, two-wheeled buggy that just went by had Major George Zimmer and banker Jacob Stoudt in it!"

CHAPTER 15

"Pass me some more of that corn, Curt."

But Curt continued to stare straight ahead, chewing his steak without hearing or replying.

"Curt!"

"Huh?"

"The corn."

"Oh." He absently reached for the dish and handed it to me. K.J. sat on a third side of the table, doing justice to his meal.

"Are you sure you couldn't have mistaken that man for someone who looked like Zimmer?" I suggested, correctly reading Curt's thoughts. "I'm constantly seeing people who remind me of someone else. There are hundreds of new people in town now. And besides, you just got a quick look at him."

But he was adamant. "There was no mistake. It was Zimmer all right."

"How can you be sure?"

"Well, first of all, I got a real good look at both of them as that buggy came toward me. And secondly, I suffered too many years under that bastard not to know him."

"But it just makes no sense for him to be here. He's not eligible for retirement, is he?"

"Not yet. But he could be on some kind of leave-of-absence. Maybe the Third Cavalry was given some relief from campaigning through the winter."

"Even assuming it was Zimmer, what would he be do-doing with Stoudt?"

Curt shrugged. "Don't know. But he always liked to

play the big operator. Wherever he goes, he likes to associate himself with the rich and influential. Even if he didn't know Stoudt before the troops came through here last fall, it'd be natural for him to worm his way into his company now."

I could see how nervous Curt had become. "Well, don't worry about it. We'll be out on our claim shortly. If it is Zimmer, we probably won't see him again. However," I added, "just to be safe, it might be a good idea if you kept your beard a while longer." The smooth, dark-brown beard rounded out Curt's lean cheeks and changed his appearance considerably. "As greedy as Zimmer is, he may have taken leave from the Army to join the gold rush himself."

I dropped the subject for the time being to concentrate on the fresh bread the waiter had just brought and help myself to more fried potatoes and onions. "It's a wonder nobody who wintered over here got scurvy," I commented half-aloud, relishing the taste of the long absent vegetables.

My elbow brushed something in my jacket pocket, and I suddenly remembered the old newspaper Jack Colcroft had given me. I took it out and unfolded it on the table. Four-month-old news was better than no news of the outside world.

K.J. finished stuffing himself, thanked us and left, while Curt and I lingered over our coffee and pipes. Curt was absorbed in his thoughts and I in my newspaper. Suddenly, an article caught my eye, and I sat upright in my chair, scanning the column quickly.

"Curt, I think I just confirmed that you did see Zimmer."

"What?"

"This newspaper is dated December thirteenth. Look at this story. General Buck and the Third Cavalry were apparently sent out from Fetterman on a winter campaign against the Cheyenne. Look . . . right here." I folded the paper and shoved it around to him. "Sounds like it may have been written by Strahorn."

Curt's eyes dropped quickly down the page, scanning the piece, reading half-aloud.

". . . struck the Cheyenne village of Dull Knife on the morning of November twenty-fifth . . . driven from the lodges . . . tipis and all equipment were burned . . . holed up at one end of the valley . . . babies frozen to death in their mothers' arms during the bitterly cold night that followed . . . many relics of Custer's Seventh Cavalry found in the tipis . . . Lieutenant McKenney and four soldiers were killed and seventeen wounded. Estimates placed the number of Cheyenne killed at twenty-two. . . ."

He looked up. "God, the whole thing is a shame. More killing. More senseless killing." He shook his head. "But what's this got to do with Zimmer being here?"

"Read on."

He glanced back at the paper. "What?" he said incredulously as his reading slowed.

". . . charges were preferred after the battle by Colonel Ranald MacKenzie against Major George Zimmer for being intoxicated on duty. General Buck would not give any details except to say this, to his knowledge, was the first time anything like this had happened while actually engaged against the hostiles . . . Major Zimmer was placed on administrative leave pending a court of inquiry into the incident."

He looked up. "So that's it. I'd sure like to get the follow-up to this story." He grinned. "The hard-drinking Major may be an ex-officer now, just like I am. Maybe there is some justice in this world, after all."

"I never doubted it for a minute." We both burst into laughter.

"Let's pay up and get out of here."

Curt snatched the bill off the table and glanced at it.

"Whew! Ten-fifty. We're going to have to go to work soon."

"I tell you what," Curt said as we left the dining room, "I don't care whether Zimmer sees me or not, now that I know he's got a lot more on his mind than turning in a deserter. Let's go get that bath and get these beards shaved."

About midafternoon we emerged clean, trimmed, shaved, and fresh-smelling. We were even wearing clean clothes and had had our boots cleaned and blacked by K.J.

"I feel about ten pounds lighter," Curt remarked. "I didn't realize how grubby I had gotten."

"Yeah. My skin feels like it's breathing again."

"Rather than you going out to Thunder Valley alone to get our camp in shape, why don't we both go, in case we run into any trouble—like claim jumpers. We can leave in the morning and come back the next day. Our animals really need the exercise, and I doubt if Cathy and Wiley could get here before we get back. Even if they do, we can leave word with Bundy to have them wait. What do you think?"

"Great idea. We've got enough money left between us to get a few provisions together, if this flood of people hasn't cleaned out the stores already."

The rest of the day was spent in selecting our supplies and redeeming and packing our horse and mules from the livery stable. They were heavy and unruly from inactivity. As we retrieved our own animals, I remarked to Curt that Floyd Mortimer must be back in town, since his horse was in the stable and his made-to-order wagon was in the back of the building.

We headed for Thunder Valley at daybreak the next morning, and I was holding my breath as we got closer to it, for fear we would find someone had worked the claim in our absence. But we were relieved to find my fears unfounded. The only signs of life we found were deer tracks and the marks of various small animals near the creek. Our tent had about half blown down or collapsed from the weight of heavy snow, but we got everything back in good order before dark. While cleaning up the camp, sewing the ripped canvas, cutting some new tent poles, storing our food and gear, I was constantly tempted to stop and do a little panning, but resisted, knowing I would not be able to get back to my chores.

We cooked some bacon and beans over our campfire that evening and slept in our tent again. After several months away, it was good to be home. Before starting back for Deadwood the next morning, we checked our claim markers to be sure they were intact and easily recognizable.

We got back to Deadwood the next afternoon and stabled our animals. One stage had come in since our departure, but the Jenkinses were not aboard, Bundy told us. We knew they couldn't have gotten here that quickly, anyway, so we went to get a beer from Burnett. Even in midafternoon the Golden Eagle was crowded, and Burnett was very busy, so he was unable to visit with us. But as I looked around the crowded room for a table, I spotted Floyd Mortimer in the back of the long room, deep in conversation with two men at one of the tables.

"The man must have some other source of income than his elixir," I remarked to Curt as we finally gave up trying to find a seat and stood at the bar. "He'd have a lot of potential customers right now if he were out there pushing the stuff."

We were halfway through our second beer when a yell from outside alerted us that a stage was arriving. About a third of the men in the saloon started outside to meet it. Even in a boom town the arrival of a stage is a big event, primarily because it brings the mail.

By the time we arrived at the Wells Fargo depot, the mud-spattered Concord coach was already discharging its cargo of humanity. And a cargo it was. I was surprised the coach's leather thoroughbraces had been able to withstand the load.

The driver and Chuck Bundy were in the middle of a crowd of passengers and bystanders. I could hear the driver talking excitedly and some of the others interrupting and trying to talk at the same time. I heard a voice mention Sheriff Pierce's name, but before I could speculate on anything, Cathy and Wiley came running toward us to hug us and grip our hands.

"By golly, you and Matt look thin," Wiley remarked,

finally stepping back to take a good look at us. "Pickin' musta been mighty lean here last winter."

"You don't know the half of it," Curt assured him. "We'll tell you all about it later."

By contrast, Wiley had filled out and looked strong and healthy. And Cathy looked even better than I remembered her, dressed in her pale gray wool skirt and matching jacket. She was hatless, and her dark brown hair was swept back from her face and held by a clasp on each side and fell loose past her collar. After the initial hug and kiss, Curt, even though he talked to Wiley too, had eyes only for Cathy.

"How was the trip up? You really made excellent time."

"Long and tiresome. The train was delayed twice by washouts. Thought we'd never get to Cheyenne. And then we were stuck there for a week before we could get passage on one of the inbound stages, they were so full," Wiley answered. "Right after we sent you the telegram, we got aboard one."

"I can't wait to get out of these clothes and into something comfortable," Cathy said with a grimace.

"Let's get your luggage and go, then. When we got your telegram, we rented you a room near ours."

"Thought all the rooms would have been rented, from the looks of this crowd," Wiley commented.

"Most of these pilgrims are in here on a shoestring, and can't afford boom-town prices," Curt said. "Which reminds me: we need to get back on our claim as soon as you get rested up; our money is nearly gone."

"Don't worry about that for a while," Wiley said. "After they settled up our father's estate, Cathy and I inherited enough to keep us for a time, provided we don't go out and blow it."

"We got one helluva welcome back to the Hills on the way up," Wiley said as we started for the hotel.

"How's that?"

"Got held up."

"They hit an inbound stage?"

"Maybe thought the passengers were carrying a lot of

valuables or money. Anyway, he never got a chance to find out. It was a lone gunman with a hood over his head. I was ridin' up top with about four others, to give the women a sheltered seat inside, and I got a perfect view. He rode out of the trees at the side of the road just as the horses were nearing the top of a long upgrade."

"Sounds like the same method as the others," Curt remarked.

"So anyway, this rider throws down on us with a Winchester and yells for the driver to pull up. The horses were already at a slow walk."

"What about the shotgun messenger?"

"There wasn't one. They were tryin' to save room for passengers. And besides, there was some talk at the Wells Fargo station that they'd never hit an inbound stage. So the driver—Rob Ellsworth was his name—pulled back on the reins and raised his right leg to step on the brake lever. Well, sir, while his leg was still in the air, there was this terrific roar, and that gunman was blown right out of his saddle. He was in another world before he hit the ground. Scared the hell out of all of us on top, it was so unexpected. And the horses, too. They jumped and plunged, and Rob just gave 'em the reins, cracked his whip over their heads, and we took off, with us topside passengers grabbing for the iron rail to keep from bein' pitched off. Old Rob never looked back, just as though it was the most natural thing in the world and happened every day. Turns out he'd been held up a few times before, especially when he drove for Wells Fargo a few years back in California. It was then he got the idea of strapping a shotgun inside his pants leg with the trigger wired up the inside of his clothes to his right hand. When he lifted his leg to apply the brake, he aimed his leg at the rider and pulled the wire."

"So that's what all the commotion was about with the driver and Bundy just now."

"Yeah."

"I just saw Sheriff Pierce saddle a horse and ride out with several men."

"Reckon he's still alive?" Curt wondered. "If so, he may be the first lead anybody's gotten to this band of gold robbers."

"Since he was ridin' alone and robbed a coach going the wrong way he may have been operating on his own" I suggested.

" 'Course, if he's dead, it won't matter much, unless he's carrying something that shows his identity."

"There's not a chance he's alive," Wiley said with a tone of finality. "That blast hit him square in the chest from no more than ten or twelve feet. He'll be a mess when they find him."

"When did this happen?" I asked.

"Less than an hour back."

A short time later we were all seated in the Golden Eagle catching up on the news. Cathy was dressed casually in soft doeskin breeches and boots. Her pale green-and-white checked shirt was equally tasteful and well fitted.

"I knew I was coming back, so I invested in some decent clothes in Louisville, and then had these pants made in Cheyenne," she replied when Curt commented on how good she looked. "Women's clothes are totally impractical in this country, but at least these fit, and they're not just small-size men's clothes."

Somehow, her sitting there in buckskins drinking in a saloon full of men did not detract from her femininity in the least. She was a far cry from someone like Calamity Jane. She still had that fetching habit of tossing her glossy, dark brown hair back from her face every now and then. Her long-absent smile brightened our table, and by the look of things, Curt's heart.

"We got about three hundred dollars more out of our claim after you left and before the weather shut us down," Curt was saying. "And nothing's happened until we went out there yesterday to clean up the place."

"For the first time in my life, I have enough money that I don't have to worry about where my next several meals are coming from," Wiley said. "Although I'd rather have my father alive and not have his inheritance. But

I'm still itching to get my hands on a shovel or a pan and get back at that gold."

"Well, it's been locked up for you all winter in the ice and snow," I said. "Nobody's bothered it."

"So, what did you two do with all your time this winter?" Cathy asked. "Probably chased these saloon girls when you weren't gambling," she added, her eyes sparkling mischievously.

"Have you taken a close look at some of these girls?" Curt asked. "We weren't that bored."

She laughed. "Wiley found out that all his old girl friends were married or gone, and things had changed a lot since he was last home. But we did get reacquainted with all our kin. It was good to be back in civilization again. We had a good visit and a good rest. How was your winter?"

Curt filled them in on our nearly fatal hunting trip. Even though he glossed over some of the details of the experience, I saw Cathy's face pale slightly as he spoke.

"But we're all healed up fine, and none the worse for it," I assured her. "And we did get a buffalo, even though I heard some of the people complaining that it was old and that the meat was tough and stringy. They even skinned him and made a good buffalo robe for me and Curt."

We all ordered another beer, and the conversation drifted on to other things. I noticed that Wiley was drinking strictly beer, and was leaving the hard liquor alone.

We told them of our suspicions about the stage robberies, and about Major George Zimmer's showing up in Deadwood.

"There was a lot about that battle in the papers," Wiley said. "And of course, they jumped on the scandal of Zimmer drinking on duty and really blew that up."

"What exactly happened?" Curt asked.

"As I remember the story, Zimmer ordered a charge against some Cheyenne braves who were entrenched in one end of the valley. His men were beaten back, and several of them were unnecessarily killed and wounded.

That's when Colonel MacKenzie discovered he was pretty well drunk. Zimmer claimed he'd just had a nip or two to ward off the extreme cold."

"What's happened since? We just found out about it this week from an old newspaper."

"I haven't really been following it, but I believe the court-martial hasn't been held yet. He requested a leave of absence and was granted it, and the court-martial was postponed—I think by some political string-pulling. Anyway, I believe I read where the trial will be later this summer, so he's still technically in the army. But it doesn't look good for him, from what I gather."

"He'll use every trick in the book to get out of this," Curt said. "The longer he can delay it, the better chance he's got. He may be here to make plans for the day he's kicked out of the army. There's plenty of money floating around this town and in the Hills."

"I guess I'd be doing the same thing if I were in his boots," I remarked. "I almost feel sorry for the man."

Curt gave me a peculiar look and started to say something, but Wiley cut in with, "Well, I don't. How many men do you suppose would be alive today if it weren't for him? How many do you reckon he's run crazy or caused to desert? I believe the old boy is finally getting a little dose of his own medicine. And I didn't even have to serve under him." We both looked at Curt, but he had apparently decided not to voice an opinion.

I noticed the sun had disappeared behind the hills and it was growing dark outside. The room was becoming crowded, and I could barely hear the sound of the hurdy-gurdy over the hum of voices.

Two billiard tables had just been added at the extreme rear of the deep room. Apparently ordered some months ago, they had arrived on one of the first bull trains from Pierre. The clicking of the ivory balls added to the noise of glassware and rattling poker chips. Every time someone opened the door, the draft stirred the heavy haze of smoke that hung below the high ceiling.

"I'm about to starve," Wiley said suddenly. "Haven't

eaten a decent meal in three days. You know how the food is at those way stations."

"No sooner suggested than done," Curt agreed, pushing his chair back. "Let's go. The time just got away from me."

Just then the door opened, and in walked Floyd Mortimer, silver hair shining in the light of the oil lamps. He paused just inside to let his eyes adjust to the glare, and I saw him look quickly over the room. He was dressed in a natty coat and vest with a cravat. He wore no visible side arms.

"Coming, Matt?" I was suddenly aware that Curt was talking to me.

Wiley followed my stare. "Why, isn't that the snake-oil drummer?"

"Yes. You three go ahead. I'm not hungry just now. I'll meet you back here after supper. I want to talk to Mortimer a minute."

"Okay, see you in about an hour. We'll be down at the Grand Central if you decide to join us."

"Right."

Mortimer had elbowed his way up to the bar, and Burnett was drawing him a beer. He took a deep draft of it, then turned back toward the room and leaned back with his elbows on the bar.

"Mister Mortimer! Mister Mortimer! Over here." I waved him toward my table. I could see the puzzled look on his face as he drew up a chair.

"I believe you have the advantage of me, sir," he said, offering his hand. I gripped it in a firm handshake.

"Matt Tierney, Mister Mortimer. You looked as though you were looking for a place to sit."

"I am pretty tired. Spent a good part of the day at Crook City trying to peddle my wares. It's a shame I have to stoop to sleight-of-hand magician's tricks to draw a crowd. I'm afraid I'm getting a little old for this type of life. Too bad it took me so many years to discover my elixir."

I looked at him carefully. In spite of his claims of age and his wavy silver hair, his skin and hands belonged to

a man no older than his early forties. I decided to gamble.
I glanced around to be sure no one was overhearing us.
But the din of conversations and background noise
masked anything we said.

"What's your real game, Mortimer? You're no more a
drummer than I am."

He looked up sharply at me and his florid complexion
deepened several shades of red. "What do you mean?"

"Just what I said. Who are you, anyway?"

"In this country, a man calls another a liar at his own
risk, Tierney. A man's background is always his own."

"No offense, but I just have you pegged as too intelligent to be a legitimate snake-oil drummer."

"Elixir."

"All right, elixir. I'm from Ireland, some years back,
and I've heard some windy characters and tall tales in
my time, but you somehow don't ring true to me. There's
more to you than just another itinerant snake-oil quack.
You may have been paying K.J. out of the goodness of
your heart, but you've been doing a lot of strange snooping around. Besides, unless you have some other financing,
I don't think you could live and dress and drive the rig
you have on what you've sold here."

He looked thoughtful but not upset, so the flattery had
had some effect. When he spoke, his tone was not hostile.

"Who are you to be asking so many questions, Mister
Tierney? If I'm to tell you anything about myself, I believe, sir, that you should return the favor."

"I'm just a transplanted Irishman from Chicago who
was with the Third Cavalry on their campaign last year
in the capacity of a reporter."

"Ahhh, a reporter. Now I remember you. You've been
working as a reporter for a paper here in town. I've seen
your by-line."

"I'm not working there anymore. But I guess you could
say I have a reporter's instinct. It never leaves you,
whether you're working or not." I smiled at him, trying
to put him at ease. "And there are a lot of interesting
people in this town. For instance, I'd like to know more
about the banker, Jacob Stoudt."

He chose to ignore my remark. "There's an open table in the back. Care for a game of billiards?"

"Sure."

The table was next to the back door, and we reached it just before two other men. Mortimer said no more, and I didn't press the issue as we chalked our cues and started the game. Obviously, he was not talking, but from his attitude I knew my hunch was right about his not being a real drummer. I leaned against the back wall and watched him bend over the table in the light of the low-hanging lamp. The man was a real mystery, a challenge to me, and I was determined to find out more about him. I fancied that I still had the Gaelic gift of charm and gab that was every Irishman's birthright. The way I figured it, I had made some headway; he hadn't ignored me and walked away.

I took a shot, missed, and stepped back as he chalked his cue and leaned over the table, back to the door, to line up a shot.

I heard the muzzle blast and was showered with broken glass at the same instant. I ducked quickly and scrambled along the floor to get the table between me and the door. Out of the corner of my eye I saw Mortimer also hit the floor. I finally got to cover and yanked my gun. The room behind me was in confusion as the men scrambled to their feet or dove for cover. I stared hard at the black, jagged hole where the glass in the back door had been. But there were no more shots.

"Hey, Floyd!"

No answer.

"Mortimer!" I crawled cautiously around the end of the pool table. He lay on the floor where he had fallen, his hand pressed to his left side. He looked up and moaned softly. Sweat beads were popping out on his face, and his face had gone white. Just as I looked, his jaw fell slack and he rolled over on his back, unconscious, on the shards of broken glass. His coat fell open, and his hand fell away from a bright, bloody spot on his vest.

CHAPTER 16

"How're you feeling?" I asked Floyd Mortimer as the doctor left the room, closing the door behind him.

"Sore as a boil," he grimaced, trying to prop himself higher on the pillows. The doctor had just checked, cleaned, and rebandaged the wound in Mortimer's side. It was late the next afternoon in my room at the Merchants Hotel.

"You say you didn't see anybody outside?" Mortimer asked.

"It was a minute or so before a few of us went out back. We didn't want to rush out there blind and maybe get ourselves gunned down. Whoever it was had plenty of time to get away. I had you carried up here."

"Thanks."

"You're mighty lucky."

"Lucky?" He arched his gray eyebrows over the long, straight nose. "Lucky to be shot?"

"Lucky it just barely clipped your side. Otherwise, we might be planning your funeral right now. That bullet went right through the muscle, the doctor said. Missed all vital organs and the intestines. The doctor says you'll be out of action for at least a couple of weeks. But if infection doesn't set in, you should be good as new after that."

He groaned and lay back, closing his eyes. "A couple of weeks. Oh, no!"

"You don't seem too grateful for a man who's just missed death by a few inches."

"Oh, I really appreciate what you did for me," he

hastened to add. "It's just that I hate to be laid up that long."

"Don't worry. Your rig will be waiting for you. And if it's money you're worried about, I can lend you whatever you need until you get back on your feet. You can even cancel your room reservation at the Grand Central and stay here. I'll keep it rented; we're going out to our claim and won't need it."

"Thanks." He gave me a wan smile.

"Any idea who would want to shoot you?"

"Might have been an accident," he replied unconvincingly.

"You can't really believe that."

"He might have been shooting at you."

"When he fired, I was leaning against the wall. He couldn't have even seen me from outside the door."

"Could've been a stray shot from up on the hill behind the saloon. Maybe somebody hunting."

"In the dark? Nope. We dug the bullet out of the pool table. It was a slug from a forty-five. Besides, I heard the shot right outside the door when he fired."

"He must have had mighty poor aim if he almost missed me from that range," Mortimer remarked.

"Either that, or the glass deflected the bullet slightly."

He didn't reply. He appeared to be distracted by something else. He glanced around the room and licked his dry lips.

"Would you pour me some water?" I complied. After he had drunk, he asked, "Where are your friends?"

"They went down to eat supper. They should be back in about a half hour. They'll be bringing you something to eat."

"You're a reporter, aren't you?" he asked, pursuing his own line of thought.

"I was. I'm not now."

"You've been very kind to me and I feel I ought to tell you something. You've earned the right to know more about me, but I can't confide in you without your word that it will not be written up in any paper."

"You've got my word."

"Before I was shot last night, you were asking me questions about my background, and if I were really a medicine man. What made you suspect I wasn't?"

I told him about K.J. and the strange errands he told me he had done for Mortimer. "And I also suspected a man couldn't make as much money as you appeared to have by running a medicine show."

"You're right. I'm a special agent for Wells Fargo. I was sent here to see if I could somehow put a stop to all these stage robberies. The company is losing a lot of money and a lot of its reputation. I thought my guise as a drummer would allow me to talk to everyone and mingle freely without being suspected."

"Ah, so that's it." I pulled a straight-backed chair near the bed and sat down. "Who else knows who you are?"

"Well, Chuck Bundy, of course. But as far as I know, he's the only one. And now you. But the more people who find out, the less effective I'll be. I'm only telling you now because I owe you a debt."

"I realize that. I'd like your permission to tell my partners. They're completely trustworthy, and I believe we might be of some help to you."

"If you really mean that, I may take you up on your offer. Looks like I'll be laid up here for a while."

"You say Bundy's the only one who knows your real identity?"

"I thought so until last night. Whoever shot me apparently knows who I am. So, I guess it doesn't really matter who knows now, if my enemies are on to me."

"Any idea who's back of all this?"

"Not really. But all the leads I've traced so far point to a character known as Cassius 'Stumpy' McCoy and his gang."

"Name sounds vaguely familiar."

"It should. He and his boys have made themselves the terror of every boom town and mining camp since the war. Their style is to let prospectors and miners sweat for gold so they can lift it. Occasionally, they'll jump a lone prospector on his claim, but their specialty is hitting stage lines with coin and currency, payrolls, bullion shipments, and the like. The gang has varied in number from five to a dozen over the years, and various members have been caught or killed, but Stumpy just keeps going."

"He's never been caught?"

"Once. But he escaped while he was being taken by train to court in Denver. That was three years ago. He had all but dropped out of sight until last year, when all the robberies on stages going out of the Hills began to smell like his operation again."

"Why's he called Stumpy?"

"Lost four fingers and half of the thumb off his left hand in an explosion. He was setting charges in a mine at the time. Story has it that when he recovered, he swore he would never work for wages again. His few defenders claim that's what set him on a life of crime. Figured to get his gold the easy way."

"Sounds like quite an opponent. He must be pretty smart to have been caught only once."

"Smart? I don't really think so. Slippery, maybe. Canny, wily, instinctively cunning perhaps. But I've tracked him and studied his habits long enough over the years to believe he's not all that intelligent."

"Well," I remarked with a slight smile, leaning back and crossing my legs, "whatever he's got apparently works; he's managed to elude you so far."

He yawned widely as the sedative the doctor had given him began to take effect. "Luck. Incredible luck. You wouldn't believe the number of times we've almost had him, and he's managed through some unexpected stroke of sheer luck, to get away. That's what bothers me about these robberies."

"What's that?"

"I get the feeling that someone else is on the inside of this case—someone tipping the gang about these treasure coaches. It's my theory the gang is robbing the passenger coaches at random just for loose change. But I really feel there is some smarter organizer behind the big robberies. They show too much finesse for Stumpy. The wheels of the machinery are too well oiled. Every possible problem appears to have been thought out in advance:

the place, the time of day or night, which robber does what—and they disappear so completely afterward. The only way this much planning can be done in advance is for the gang to know exactly what and who they are attacking. Those coaches we've had outriders on have either been allowed to go by, or the outriding guards have been intercepted and killed, or stripped and set walking in their long johns."

As he spoke, I felt as if I were listening to another man in Mortimer's body. Gone was the red-faced, bombastic medicine show drummer. This man was cool, collected, and businesslike.

"What were you going to do?" I asked.

"I had that kid, K.J., do some snooping for me," he replied without answering my question directly, "and found that at least two men who are known members of Stumpy's gang were here in Deadwood recently. In fact, they were staying at the Grand Central. But they've gone now. I tried to trail one of them, but lost him in the rocks after we'd gone about ten miles. I stayed out a couple more days trying to pick up his tracks or some sign, but no deal."

He paused for another drink of water, and I could see he was growing noticeably weaker and sleepier. I quickly filled him in on the reasons for my suspicion of the banker. And without involving Wilder, I told him of Major Zimmer.

"That only confirms my suspicions of Jacob Stoudt," he replied, nodding. "I didn't have any suspects except McCoy when I first came here. But it's really amazing what information you can pick up by casual conversation. People don't realize they're telling you anything, but little tidbits gathered here and there add up. But this Major Zimmer—I don't know." He shrugged. "Probably just a business associate. No reason to suspect him. Stoudt deals with a lot of high-ranking people in his line of work."

"Are you sure Bundy is above suspicion?"

"Absolutely. Not a finer man in the company. I'd trust him with my life—and have a couple of times in the past."

"What about that man who was shot in the holdup attempt yesterday?"

"I rode out with Sheriff Pierce to see the body just after the stage came in with the news. We recognized him from some Wanted posters as a suspected member of Stumpy's gang. But his pockets were turned inside out and his horse was missing. Of course, his horse just might have wandered off, or headed back to where he came from. We weren't able to track him more than half a mile. But there were tracks of another horse, too. Someone definitely got to the body and removed any and all additional evidence we might have picked up from it, including weapons. They just left the body for us to bury."

Just then there was a knock on the door, and Curt, Wiley, and Cathy walked in. "A little nourishment for the patient," Wiley announced, sweeping a white linen cover off the tray he was carrying. "Steak, taters, corn—the whole thing."

Mortimer managed a wan smile. "Thanks. I really appreciate it. But I'm not too hungry just now."

"Well, eat what you can, and we'll take care of the rest." Wiley propped the tray on a pillow on Floyd's lap.

While he picked at the food and drank a little of the coffee, I briefed the three on what Mortimer had told me. Mortimer added a comment now and then.

"There's one other thing I haven't mentioned," Mortimer said, finally pushing the tray aside. "And I may need your help keeping an eye on this while I'm laid up. Over the past few months I've discovered that one particular room in the Grand Central is occupied off and on by one of Stumpy's gang. I thought I recognized the man in the saloon one night. To be certain, I hired K.J. to deliver a newspaper to his room to see if he had a scar on his upper arm. When he checked out, I followed him. Tracked him for two days in the hills. I don't know if he knew he was being followed, or if he took a roundabout way just as a precaution, but I finally lost him not more than ten miles from Deadwood."

"That must have been when I was looking for you.

Stoudt left town at the same time, because I was looking to interview him when I couldn't find you."

"I was pretty disgusted when I lost him. He just vanished. One minute he was there, and the next minute he was gone. He went over a ridge, and I came over the same ridge maybe a half-mile back of him, and he wasn't there. The ground was grass and rocky shale. What little sign he left in that open valley just disappeared. Maybe an expert tracker could've followed him a little farther, I don't know. But he had no time to ride out of that valley or into any cover before I topped the ridge behind him. In fact, when I didn't see him immediately, I stopped in the trees for a while and just studied the valley. Thought he might be waiting in ambush for me. Although, for the life of me, I didn't see a place big enough to hide him and his horse.

"But, to get on with what I started to say . . . I got back to town and got to checking around quietly. Had to 'borrow' the registration book at the Grand Central late one night and look it over. It looked like room 204 over the past year had been occupied more than twenty times by the same man, who signed in as 'Jason Thomas'—very likely an alias. Later, by a little discreet questioning of the day clerk I got some information I could piece together. He recalled what this Jason Thomas looked like. It was the same man K.J. had checked for a scar on his arm—a man I knew as Joe Grimes. No telling what his real name is. The man was a frequent guest in the hotel, and usually occupied the same room—two-oh-four. The clerk remarked that as much as this man came and went, he must be a traveling salesman. Said Mister Thomas was there so often, it probably would have been cheaper for him to rent a room by the month, rather than paying three-fifty a night."

He paused to take another sip of water before continuing. I noticed his florid complexion had paled. The light in the room was fading as dusk settled outside. I got up and lighted the lamp as Mortimer continued.

"The whole thing didn't make sense to me, and after puzzling over it for a while, I just dismissed it as insig-

Dakota Gold 165

nificant. But then one night at dinner an idea hit me. I had to bribe the desk clerk to get the information, and give him some cock-and-bull story as to why I wanted to know, but he gave me the dates over the past year that Jason Thomas had checked out of the hotel. I compared these dates with Bundy's records and found that in twenty-two out of twenty-five cases, his checkout dates were either the day of, or the day before, a stage robbery."

Cathy, Wiley, Curt, and I looked at each other without speaking or breaking the spell that was settling over the room. Mortimer's usually strong voice was still intense but growing weaker in volume as he talked.

"I guessed that someone had to be tipping him about the treasure shipments."

"I thought those treasure shipments were pretty general knowledge, and it was just that they couldn't stop the robbers."

"It was some of both. We tried several means of preventing any robbers getting the gold from the coach, and when that didn't work, we resorted to hiding the gold in various places or taking the gold out of the Hills in erratic, unscheduled, secret shipments, not necessarily on the coaches. But they were waiting for every shipment, no matter how secret we thought it was. Once, the gold was even hidden in small sacks inside the seats and wall panels of the coach. The driver told me they went right to it, as though they had put it there themselves. Somebody here in town has to be tipping Jason Thomas, who then rides out to wherever the gang is holed up and gives them the word."

"Why not just grab Thomas?"

"Can't arrest him without some kind of evidence of wrongdoing. And besides, he's just a messenger. We need to get the informant and Stumpy—plus whoever else may be behind it—or it will just continue."

"Well, if we can help you in any way, just say the word," Curt said.

"I don't know about the other stage line, but Wells Fargo is not going to make a treasure shipment for a week or two at least. Maybe longer. The claims and the mines are just now opening up for the season, so it'll be a little while before the gold starts coming in in quantity. Then it has to be smelted into ingots. I'm working on a plan, and I may need your help, but it won't be until just before we're ready to make our first shipment. By then I should be well. But right now I can hardly keep my eyes open."

"Let's get out of here and let him get some sleep. He's lost quite a bit of blood," I said, waving the others toward the door.

"Sorry to be taking your bed," he mumbled sleepily as Cathy helped him slide down in bed and arranged his pillows.

"Don't worry about it," Wiley said. "I just checked with Missus Hayes, and tomorrow we'll be carrying you up there. That's where you'll get some real nursing." Wiley retrieved the tray and we headed toward the door.

"It's a little early for our bedtime, but Cathy and Wiley will be bedding down on the floor in here later to keep an eye on you," Curt told him.

But I don't think Mortimer even heard him.

CHAPTER 17

Two days later we were back on our claim in Thunder Valley, just as if five months had not intervened. Things were the same—the same, that is, with two exceptions. Instead of fall, spring was here in all its glory. And second, we now had company. Inevitably, other prospectors had found Thunder Valley, and claims were staked above and below our discovery claims, but no one had bothered our stretch of creek. Our sluice box had been damaged but with a few repairs was back in operation.

I didn't want to pry, but Cathy and Wiley seemed to have a considerable amount of money from their inheritance. They insisted on paying for all the supplies we needed, and settled up our bills at the hotel and the livery stable. They even bought us another two horses with saddles. I didn't ask them how much they had, and they didn't mention a figure, so Curt and I let it go at that. We were both pretty short on funds and had to depend on new gold finds to make our stake. Curt and I decided between ourselves to make sure we reimbursed the Jenkinses so the gold and expenses would eventually be divided four equal ways.

Before leaving Deadwood, we had taken Floyd Mortimer to convalesce at Mrs. Hayes's place. Even though she already had K.J., two orphaned teenage boys, one mistreated wife, and her usual supply of itinerant prostitutes under her wing, she welcomed the wounded drummer. She didn't want to accept any money for his care, but we finally forced it on her anyway and told her we would be back in a week or two to check on him.

It didn't take long for the fine, golden grains in the tail of the sluice to put Mortimer, Deadwood, the stage robberies, and everything else out of my mind. Our own cleanup started at about a half-ounce a day and varied upward to an ounce and a half. The word had spread about our valley, and shortly claims number two and three below our discovery were staked. I tried to get an idea of how well our immediate neighbors on the creek were doing, but those above us were experienced, close-mouthed prospectors fresh from the Montana goldfields at Virginia City, and were not sharing any information with us. The party immediately below were neophytes from Iowa who were excitedly proclaiming every bit of color they panned. Hearing their cries of joy, one would think they had found the pot of gold at the end of the rainbow. In truth, it probably seemed so to them, judging from their dirt-poor appearance. They were as open and trusting and delighted as children. They often visited our camp and examined our gear and our sluice box, declaring that as soon as they had panned enough gold, they were going into Deadwood, pay off their bills, trade in their two bony mules, and buy some lumber to build a rocker of their own.

The days were warm and pleasant, and the nights delightfully cool. An early, warm spring had set in without the usual spring rains. After two weeks Curt and Wiley went out hunting and brought back a fine buck, whose meat we shared with the Iowans, who appeared to be half starved.

"I've lost all track of time since we've been back out here," Wiley declared as we sat around our campfire the night after they had returned from their successful hunt. "What day of the week is it, anyway?"

"Friday, I think," Cathy replied, staring into the fire and apparently doing some mental calculations. "And this is late April, but I'm not sure of the date. We should probably get back to town and check on Mister Mortimer."

"I know," Curt replied. "He should be pretty well recovered by now. How much gold have we accumulated so far?"

"It was right at twenty-six and a half ounces when I weighed it last night," Wiley replied. "But I doubt if we got even a half ounce today. I hope it's not beginning to play out." He grinned. "Just when all this shoveling has about gotten me into shape."

"It's so pleasant out here, I almost hate to go back," Curt said, poking at the fire with a stick. He caught the end of the stick afire and proceeded to light his pipe. We were all bathed in a red glow that reflected off the white tent wall a few feet behind us.

"We may not want to go back, but if Stumpy McCoy's gang isn't stopped, we'll probably not get our gold out of the Hills safely," I said.

"We're not being paid to chase robbers," Wiley grumbled.

"Maybe not, but Mortimer told me there was a reward for anyone who helps catch, kill, or convict whoever's behind it. He's not eligible for the reward himself, since he's a Wells Fargo employee."

"How much reward?" Wiley asked. "I may get a little more public-spirited if it will fatten my poke."

"One thousand dollars, gold."

"Count me in," Wiley decided. "Unless there's a chance I'll get my hide ventilated."

"Mortimer mentioned he had a plan in mind, but he didn't elaborate," Curt said.

"And we did promise to help him," Cathy added, "even when there was no mention of a reward."

"Why don't we go into town tomorrow, then?" Curt suggested. "We can take our gold in for smelting."

"All right by me. Think there's any need for one of us to stay behind to guard against claim jumpers?"

"Aw, to hell with that," Wiley said. "If anyone jumps this claim, they'll have to work just as hard as we did to get a little bit of gold. Besides, we'll probably only be gone a couple of days. Those Iowans below us seem like honest folk. We could ask them to keep an eye on it for us. Maybe even pay them a little for their trouble."

"Sounds good to me," I agreed.

*   *   *

By noon the next day we were back in Deadwood, had entrusted our gold to Wells Fargo, and were sitting with Mortimer in the Golden Eagle Saloon, munching on cheese, crackers, and pickles, and drinking beer. The sun was blazing down outside and a hot wind was blowing—more like late June than April. Even at this early hour, the saloon was about half full, and Burnett was busy behind the bar, serving drinks and weighing out dust.

"Yessir, best nursing care I've ever had," Floyd Mortimer was saying.

"Told you she was good," I asserted. "Missus Hayes probably put some mountain remedy on you that was a quick-cure."

"I don't know about that, but it sure as hell healed up fast and without any complications. I was up and around in a week."

"Any new developments on your research?" Curt asked in a lower voice, glancing around to be sure we were out of earshot of the next table.

"I finally got a chance to talk to Bundy the other night," Mortimer replied quietly. "And we concocted a scheme we think might smoke out whoever's behind all this."

"Tell us about it."

The tall, silver-haired agent leaned forward on both elbows and spoke intensely. "In order to have a chance of working, this plan has to have absolute secrecy. Right now, Bundy and I are the only ones who know about it, since we're the ones who made it up. Bundy is not even going to tell Sheriff Pierce about it, or wire his counterpart at our office in Cheyenne. Now, I'm going to tell you, mainly because I need your help. I'm healed up pretty well, but I still haven't got all my strength back. And, second, I know I can trust you four. Here's what we want to do: Nearly everybody in town knows that a good amount of gold has accumulated at the Wells Fargo office for smelting into ingots for shipment to the railroad. Whoever's waylaying these shipments knows that we'll have to take out a load soon. We want to let it slip that the gold will go out by wagon, under four armed guards at night. We give the grapevine time to get the news to the robbers so they can lay their plans. Then, the evening the secret shipment is supposed to go out, we let the word slip to Stoudt, possibly by way of K.J., that there is no gold on that wagon, that it's really just a trap for the drygulchers. One or two of you must stick close to Stoudt and watch every move he makes after that. If he's innocent, there's no harm done and he's none the wiser. Also, I need to have someone keep an eye on Jason Thomas, or whatever his real name is. He's back in his room at the Grand Central. I may take that job, since I'm the only one of us who knows what he looks like. If my suspicions are correct, Stoudt or Thomas should lead us to wherever the gang is hidden out. With any luck at all we should be able to grab the ringleaders."

"That all seems simple enough in theory," Wiley said, "but it sounds like it's pretty chancy. There are too many things that could go wrong. We're not professional lawmen. If some shooting starts, one of us is liable to get killed. And that someone could be me!"

"That's a point, Floyd," Curt said. "Why wasn't Sheriff Pierce brought in on this? He represents the law in Deadwood."

"Well, he's been in on all the other plans we've made in the past. Plans that didn't work. Even though we have no reason to suspect the sheriff of complicity, we decided to eliminate everyone who had been in on the planning in the past, just to be sure there's no leak from that source. I'll admit it's dangerous, but we're getting desperate. You don't really have any direct stake in this, so you're free to say no if you want to. But something's got to be done to stop these people. The company is suffering big financial losses, and we're even having trouble keeping good drivers and guards working for us. And last, and probably least, my job may be on the line. The only thing I ask, if you decide not to go in with me on this, is to forget we ever had this little talk.

"Oh, I forgot to mention that Wells Fargo has put up a thousand-dollar reward for the capture of the robbers. I'm not eligible for this, but you would be. As I said, we've got to catch the brains behind this operation almost red-handed. We have our suspicions, but we can't arrest anyone on suspicions. We can't identify the gold after it's stolen, because all they have to do to erase all markings is melt and recast it. Even if we only get Jason Thomas and Stumpy McCoy, we should be able to force a confession about who are the brains behind the scenes."

He stopped talking and took a deep draft of his beer, then swept the moisture from the bottom of his mustache with one quick motion and leaned back in his chair.

The four of us looked silently at each other, then away. We stared away into far corners, down at our hands or the floor, lost in our own thoughts and weighing our own decisions. I was thrilled by the whole idea, and I knew Curt was not afraid, but Wiley was having second thoughts, and I was worried about the idea of having Cathy involved in this, even though I knew she was very capable of taking care of herself. I'm sure Curt had Cathy's safety in mind as well, and I could almost read on his face the thoughts of how this scheme might work or might go awry. As far as I was concerned, there was nothing more to think about. I was all for it, but I held my tongue, not wanting to influence the others. For a few seconds there was silence at our table, and I was aware of the background noise in the room—a low hum of voices, an occasional laugh, the clinking of a bottle against glass.

"Count me in," Wiley finally said. "Hell, this can't be as dangerous as some of the things I've gotten myself into in the past. And it may prove to be a damn sight more rewarding."

"I'll do it," Curt added.

Cathy and I nodded our agreement to make it unanimous.

"Good," Mortimer said. "Give me a day or two to get with Bundy and let the word leak out about this secret shipment. I'll contact you Thursday at your hotel."

The next two days we killed in town, catching up on the local news and watching the constant building going on. Hammer, saw, and axe were going all day every day. And good wages were being paid to skilled carpenters.

"A lot of these newcomers have no intention of grubbing for gold," Wiley remarked to me and Curt as the three of us stood on the boardwalk watching a new building going up across the street. The town was expanding up and down the gulch and into Whitewood Gulch. Williams Street above Main was being developed beyond Mrs. Hayes's spacious log cabin.

"You're right. They have a surer, steadier way of making a good living. If they don't get caught up in the gambling, they'll probably be better off than most of the men here," Curt remarked.

"All the good places around close to Deadwood have already been staked," Cathy added. "The Homestake Mine over at Lead is already into hard-rock mining. I hear they've really struck it there."

"Apparently, that bunch over there is hot on the trail of something, too," her brother added, pointing to a half-dozen miners shoveling dirt into buckets from a trench that ran directly under the corner of one of the Chinese wash houses. Mining law allowed anyone to pursue a vein of ore anywhere it led, and apparently this one led under the wooden structure that they had propped up on rocks and short, squared-off logs where several feet of earth had been scooped from under it. The men were taking turns carrying the buckets of ore about two hundred yards to their sluice box on the creek.

"If this summer proves to be as dry as the spring has been, those lower claims may not have enough water to wash out their gravel," Curt observed, squinting at the cloudless sky. "We haven't had any rain in over two weeks. We should be getting a lot of it this time of year, especially in these hills."

A hot wind was blowing down the gulch, kicking up the dust from all the hooves and wheels in Main Street. I could see the pines bowing and waving to the even stiffer breeze on the top of the ridge above town.

"Looks like Mortimer over there," Curt said, nodding toward a group of men diagonally across the street. Just as I looked, a figure detached itself from the group and started across the street toward us. I had to look closely to be sure it was Floyd Mortimer. He was no longer dressed as a flashy drummer. He wore dark, wrinkled pants stuffed into flat-heeled boots, a collarless white shirt, and a vest. His silver mane was covered by a low-crowned hat. There was nothing in his appearance that would make anyone look twice at him.

He came up into the shade beside us, took his hat off, and passed a hand across his forehead, wiping perspiration.

"Okay, the word is out. I've heard it around, and even spread it some myself. By now, most of the town knows the 'secret' about the big gold shipment that is supposed to go out tonight by wagon. I'm sure Stoudt has heard the story."

He paused as two men passed us on the walk.

"Yeah, I've heard some mention of it myself," I remarked.

"Now, all we have to do is plant the seed of phony information in Stoudt's mind. I've talked to K.J., and he's all excited about the idea. I've kept an eye on Stoudt for several weeks, and he's a man of unvarying habit. Every night about seven thirty, he goes into the Alhambra for two shots of whiskey and some small talk with his cronies. So, I'm almost positive he'll be there tonight. I've instructed K.J. to go in there selling his papers and interrupt this group, supposedly to sell newspapers, and then ask them if they've heard the news that didn't make the paper. Then he's to tell them that the gold shipment is phony, that it's just an elaborate trap."

"What makes you think they'll pay any attention to a kid?" Curt asked.

"Everybody in town knows K.J. And they also know that he gets wind of everything that's afoot. He's as reliable as any information they're likely to get from some other source. If they have some contact to verify this with, they'll be stumped, because K.J., Bundy, you four, and I are the only ones who know about this. I'm banking on the hunch that they'll still believe the kid has some inside information. If they ask him where he found out, he's to tell them he's sworn to secrecy about his sources. They wouldn't dare put any pressure on him for fear of calling attention to themselves."

"I sure hope this works," Curt said.

"If we're wrong about Stoudt, there'll be nothing to stop the gang from holding up the wagon."

"By the way, is there really gold on that wagon?"

"No. Only several locked express boxes full of rocks."

"What about the driver and guards? Do they know?"

"They think they're being well paid to take a load of gold bullion to Cheyenne."

"I'm hungry," Wiley said suddenly. "Why don't we go get some lunch and discuss the details."

We needed no urging.

CHAPTER 18

By 6:30 that evening we were all in our places, Curt and I and Cathy at the bar in the Alhambra, Wiley and Mortimer in the lobby of the Grand Central. Curt and I had tethered our two saddled horses to the hitching rail in front of the Alhambra, just in case they were needed.

Fortunately, the Alhambra was crowded. It was a big saloon and gambling hall, with an adjacent room, nearly as large, that served as a dance hall. The bar ran along the entire side of one room. By keeping our backs to the room, we could see what was going on behind us by way of the large, ornate mirror back of the bar. Boots propped on the brass rail, we studied the mirror over the tops of our beer mugs and waited.

At 7:10 by the big pendulum clock on the opposite wall, I spotted the bulky form of Major George Zimmer. I ducked my head and nudged Curt. He spotted him about the same time, and we leaned down low over the bar and watched Zimmer find his way to a vacant table, where he was shortly joined by another well-dressed man I didn't know. Curt and I had not removed our hats, so the light from the overhead lamps threw our faces partly in shadow.

Cathy was on the opposite side of Curt, and I saw him whisper something to her, and a minute later she unobtrusively headed for the bat-wing doors and disappeared into the night.

"I told her to go over to the Grand Central," Curt said to me, raising his voice slightly to make himself heard over the noise of the piano in the dance hall. "She

176

doesn't really look like one of the women who work here, and I didn't want to take a chance on her being recognized by Zimmer."

Promptly at 7:30 Jacob Stoudt walked in, just as Mortimer had predicted he would. He walked straight to the table where Zimmer sat, signaling to a waiter as he went. The waiter apparently knew what he wanted, because he came immediately to the bar and said something to the bartender, who reached under the bar and brought out a bottle and three shot glasses and set them on the waiter's tray.

We ordered another beer and sipped and waited. At 7:40, K.J. wandered in, a small stack of papers under one arm. He wound his way through the crowd, hawking the news, laughing, waving at friendly faces. Very casually, he worked back to Stoudt's table, and we watched intently in the mirror as Stoudt gestured impatiently at the boy. But K.J. would not be brushed off so easily as he held up a paper and said something to the black-clad banker. I was dying to be able to hear the conversation. How convincing could a ten-year-old be? Maybe because the information was coming from such a source, it would be more believable.

"If I were a betting man, my money would be riding on K.J.," Curt muttered to me, not removing his eyes from the mirror.

Finally, as if to get rid of a pest, Stoudt dug into his pocket for a coin and bought a paper. Then K.J. glanced around, and I saw him lean in among the three men conspiratorially and say something. This seemed to catch Stoudt's attention. He straightened up perceptibly, and I could see him talking intently to the boy. But K.J. shrugged, backed away, and began to hawk his papers toward the next table.

Immediately, the three men leaned their heads together and began conferring earnestly. A minute or two later, Stoudt hurriedly got up without finishing his drink, picked up his hat, and left.

"Well, here we go," I whispered to Curt as we edged toward the door after his retreating figure.

"If he's in on it, he's sure taken the bait," Curt replied.

Outside, the wind was still blowing, and we had to pause to momentarily shield our eyes from the swirling dust and get accustomed to the darkness.

"Where'd he go? We can't afford to lose him."

"There he is."

A square of light from a door being opened across the street briefly revealed Stoudt's outline as he entered the lobby of the Grand Central.

"So far, so good. Let's go."

We hurried across the street, but only casually strolled into the lobby. Stoudt was nowhere to be seen, but I caught Mortimer's eye. Cathy and Wiley were seemingly intent on a game of checkers going on between two be-whiskered miners across the room. They glanced up and nodded to us. Mortimer motioned with his head, and we moved out of range of the desk clerk's hearing.

"Upstairs," he said quietly. "I'll bet it's room 204. Jason Thomas hasn't been out of that room all night. Let's go."

He motioned for Cathy and Wiley to stay where they were and then led the way to the stairs. The wooden building had only two floors, and part of the second was devoted to a parlor, the purpose of which I never knew. But the rest of the floor was partitioned off on either side of a main hall by wooden walls that reached only about eight feet above the floor, leaving a two-foot gap to the ceiling, so every noise could be heard from room to room.

There was no one in the hall, and we walked as silently as possible on the bare floor to room 204, where we stopped on either side of the door and listened. We could hear a low hum of voices, apparently two men talking, but could not make out the words.

". . . What? Are you sure? Where did—"

"Quiet, fool! Our voices carry over these walls!" This latter was the voice of Stoudt. Mortimer looked at us and nodded silently, as if to affirm that his hunch had been right. The voices within subsided into an excited but indistinguishable mumble again, and we three pressed our ears closer to the thin pine boards. Too late, we heard the scuffing of a boot behind us. I jerked my head up and found myself staring into the big black muzzle of a forty-five.

"Fate is certainly kind to give me another chance at you two," George Zimmer said, grinning humorlessly in the dim light. In the few seconds of deadly silence that followed, the clicking of a hammer being drawn to full cock sounded even louder than the beating of my own heart in my ears. A sudden thrill of fear shot through me, and for a fleeting instant I gauged my chances of making a lunge at him in the semidarkness. But he had stopped more than six feet away, and I realized I would die before I reached him. My knees began to tremble from the unused surge of desperate energy.

"I wouldn't try that, Mr. Tierney," he said, correctly reading my thoughts. "It would give me the greatest of pleasure to gun you down where you stand. Another killing in this town wouldn't matter much. I could always say I caught you breaking into a room." Just then, the door of the room was jerked open and Stoudt glanced at all of us in surprise.

"Inside, all of you!" Zimmer hissed, motioning with the gun barrel.

Stoudt backed out of the way, and the three of us were shoved inside, Zimmer following and closing the door behind us.

"What's this?" Stoudt demanded angrily.

"Caught 'em listening outside the door," Zimmer answered.

Stoudt looked closely at the three of us. "Who are you?"

After a pause, Mortimer spoke. "We thought a friend of ours was in this room. But we heard voices and wanted to listen to be sure before we knocked."

"Lies!" Stoudt snapped.

"Clerk must have given us the wrong room number," I mumbled apologetically. "No need to draw a gun on us for an honest mistake." I was never a convincing liar, and this lame excuse sounded false in my own ears even before it was out of my mouth.

"How much did they hear?" Stoudt asked Zimmer, ignoring me.

"Don't rightly know. I came up on them just before you opened the door."

A bearded man I took to be Jason Thomas, alias Joe Grimes, came up behind us and slipped my Colt from its holster and did the same with Curt's. I could smell sweat and chewing tobacco as he passed close to me. Mortimer was not wearing a gun belt, so the outlaw patted his pockets deftly up and down and then reached inside the agent's vest and slipped a small, pearl-handled, nickel-plated revolver out of a holster under his arm. Thomas threw our guns on the bed, and the three of us were ordered to stand against the wall.

"The dark-headed one there is former-Captain Curtis Wilder, who deserted my troop in the face of a court-martial for cowardice at Slim Buttes last fall," Zimmer sneered, keeping his gun leveled at us. "The one in the corduroy vest is Matthew Tierney, ex-reporter for a Chicago paper, who was with us and who helped Wilder escape." The veins stood out on his forehead at the memory, and the whiskey-burned cheeks and nose glowed even redder in the light of the lamp on the table by the window. "I don't know who this tall, white-headed gent is."

"He's a Wells Fargo agent," Stoudt said, his voice hard.

I glanced back at Zimmer. Cruelty and dissipation showed in Zimmer's face even more than I remembered from last year. Maybe with the external discipline of Army life removed, he was sliding downhill.

But this was only a passing thought as I fixed my eyes on Stoudt. We were in a desperate situation, and he was the one who appeared to be in command here. He pulled over a chair and put one foot up on it. Leaning both elbows on his knee, he regarded us silently, apparently pondering his next move. His starched white shirt, black tie, and black suit gave him the look of a successful businessman—which he was. But the face was not that of a banker about to turn down a loan. His thick, dark hair shone in the lamplight; the heavy mustache hid his mouth completely. The dark eyes were narrow slits behind the spectacles. He stroked his square chin and stared down at the floor for a few moments while noises from the street below drifted in the open window.

He straightened up abruptly. "We'll have to get rid of them," he stated as matter-of-factly as if he were ordering someone to empty the cuspidors. "We can't take a chance on their testifying against us. There is too much at stake here. I remember these two from a stagecoach ride a few months back. I don't know what they're up to, but their curiosity has just proven to be fatal. We can't do it here." He turned to Zimmer. "Take them down the back stairs and out into the hills somewhere. If you've got an old score to settle, I imagine this is a job you'll enjoy."

Zimmer grinned.

"Jason, get out to the cavern, fast, and warn McCoy off. I hope we're not already too late to catch them."

"Right." Thomas grabbed his hat, cautiously opened the door, and then disappeared quickly.

"We've got some friends waiting for us in the lobby," Curt said. "If we're not back in a few minutes, they'll be up here looking for us."

A look of sudden concern crossed Stoudt's face, but he almost immediately relaxed. "You've been reading too many dime novels, my friend," he said.

"Take a look in the hall, just to be safe," he ordered Zimmer. Keeping his Colt leveled at us, Zimmer backed to the door and opened it a crack.

"All clear."

"Good. Get them out of here. It would be best if you could arrange it so their bodies are never found. I'll meet you back at the Alhambra. Remember, no matter how late it is, report to me there. The place is open all night."

I've never felt so helpless as I did at that moment. My palms were sweaty and my throat dry. I wondered where Wiley and Cathy were. Why hadn't they tried to warn us? But, then I realized that Zimmer had approached from the opposite end of the hallway. He had come up the back stairs from the dining room.

At least they weren't going to kill us here. We had a short reprieve. Maybe our chances of escaping or of overpowering Zimmer would be much better in the darkness outside. I glanced at Curt and Floyd. Their faces were grim and set. I wished there were some way I could communicate with them. We would just have to wait and hope for a chance. But we dared not wait too long.

"Where are your horses?" Zimmer asked.

"Down at the livery," I lied quickly.

"We're all going to take a quiet walk down the back stairs and go get them, and then take a little ride into the hills. You'll get your unloaded weapons back. If you should try anything between here and when we get out of town, I'll gun all three of you down and claim self-defense. Is that clear?"

"No," Stoudt said suddenly, overriding him. "Leave their guns here. Loaded or unloaded, I don't want to take the chance of their having weapons. If you have to shoot them in town, just make sure you kill them all and then run for it. If that should happen, I'll meet you later at the cavern."

"Okay, let's go get those horses," Zimmer said.

"The livery isn't open this time of night," Mortimer reminded him, stalling.

"You *will get* your horses," Zimmer repeated, "and we'll ride out. Now, move!"

I was nearest the door, so I was the one who reached and opened it. Just as I swung it inward, I saw Cathy standing there with a double-barreled shotgun pointed at my chest. Curt and Floyd were crowded close behind me, so for a moment we blocked the view of her from Zimmer behind us.

"Get down!" I shouted and flung Curt to one side.

Before we even hit the floor, the shotgun boomed not five feet from my head, and the lamp and the window behind it exploded in a shower of flame. There were cries of surprise and pain and curses, and then the deafening roar of a forty-five as Zimmer or Stoudt began firing back. Curt and I rolled and scrambled behind the bed. There was no hope of getting out the door, since that was where all the firing was directed. The small room was rapidly filling with powder smoke in the semidarkness. Then I realized that all the smoke wasn't from the guns. An eerie light was flickering across us, and it quickly grew brighter as flames licked up the curtains. I didn't know if anyone had been hit, and I didn't know where Mortimer was. Now I could hear a forty-five blasting from the hallway, and could see muzzle flashes beside the door casing. If that was Wiley and Cathy, they sure were making it hot for Zimmer and Stoudt, who were pinned down in here with us.

I put my mouth close to Curt's ear to make myself heard. "Our guns—on the bed. Let's get 'em."

I cautiously pushed myself up on one arm and reached onto the bed. A bullet ripped away part of the quilt next to my shoulder. The next instant, I was on the floor without the gun.

"We've got to get out of here," I panted to Curt.

"How?" he yelled back over the uproar.

I had no answer. The flames were blazing higher and were licking across the wooden ceiling while, from under the bed, I could see burning pieces of the gauze curtains dropping onto the pine floor as the fire spread.

There was a sudden lull in the shooting, but before I could venture a look, there was a rush of feet across the floor, and two figures burst out the door as Zimmer and Stoudt made a break for it. Five or six more shots followed quickly, and then the sound of running boots receded down the hallway toward the back stairs.

In the few seconds of quiet that followed, I could hear shouting in the street below and the hollow thunder of boots on the stairs at both ends of the hall. A sudden gust of wind through the broken window showered the floor with burning pieces of wood, and the room grew brighter with the loud crackling of flames. Sweat was trickling down my face from the heat and excitement.

Curt and I carefully got up.

"Matt! Curt! Where are you?"

Cathy and Wiley rushed into the room, looking wildly around.

"Oh, there you are!" Cathy was in Curt's arms instantly.

"Are either of you hit?" Wiley asked, punching the empty shells out of his Colt.

"No. Where's Floyd?"

Wiley and I spotted him on the floor at the same time. Just as we grabbed his legs and pulled him back from the sparks that were beginning to fall from the ceiling onto his clothes, he moaned and rolled over. He looked up groggily at us, then reached for the back of his neck. "Musta hit my head on the washstand when I fell."

"Probably saved your life."

"Where're Stoudt and Zimmer?" he asked suddenly.

"Gone. Busted out a minute ago while my gun was empty," Wiley said. "Let's go."

The three of us grabbed our guns off the bed, which was already ablaze.

A crowd of faces jammed the doorway, but I hardly saw them as we pushed our way through the shouting mob.

"What happened?" "Is anybody hurt?" Voices were yelling questions, but nobody paid any attention.

"What the hell's going on here?" I recognized Sheriff Pierce's voice trying to shout down the tumult and get some answers.

"Fire! Fire!" the hotel clerk was screaming. The alarm was taken up by voices down the hall, and I heard the shout being echoed by voices in the street as the four of us thundered down the back stairs, through the scattering patrons in the dining room, and out into the street.

From the front we could see the flames pouring from the window. They had already taken a hold on the roof.

The wind was still gusting along the gulch, fanning the blaze as the leaping tongues licked hungrily at the top of the adjacent building.

"FIRE!" Like a death knell from a thousand voices, that most dreaded word in all frontier towns rolled in a chorus down the Main Street of Deadwood.

CHAPTER 19

"Where did they go?" Mortimer yelled. "Quick! We can't lose them."

We frantically dodged about among the crowds of running men.

"I don't see them."

"Where are their horses?"

"Probably at the livery."

"Which one?"

"Floyd, you and Wiley and Cathy check the one at the lower end of the street, and take a look at Stoudt's house on the way," Curt ordered. "Matt, come with me and we'll check the livery at the upper end of Main."

We split without another word, Curt and I running up the middle of the street, scanning every passing face and the walks on both sides for some sign of the fugitives. We had to fight our way through the tide of humanity, both afoot and on horseback, that was sweeping down the street toward the fire.

"Curt, let's get our horses. We may need them."

Just as we turned back toward the Alhambra, I spotted our Morgan over the heads of the crowd. I looked again to be sure. He was still saddled, but riderless, and was moving at a walk away from the fire, breasting the tide of townspeople. I thought he had pulled his reins loose in the excitement, but just then he jerked his head up and his rein was taut! He was being led!

"Curt, there they are! With our horses!"

The crowd was quickly growing denser as we tried to shove our way through the mass of bodies. The Morgan and our other horse were about thirty yards from us.

But reaching them was like trying to run in a dream—no matter how we struggled, we could barely make headway against the mob that was converging on the fire.

The crowd thinned for a second or two, and I caught a glimpse of Stoudt and then Zimmer before the gap closed and they were lost to sight.

"I don't think they saw us," I said to Curt.

"Maybe not, but they know we're close behind 'em somewhere. Dammit!"—he burst out in frustration—"they know we can't use our guns in this crowd. That's a pretty slick trick. They know they're safe as long as they don't mount up."

We shouldered our way along, guns drawn, our eyes riveted on the heads of our horses that stayed always ahead of us. But less than thirty seconds later, we saw the pair break free of the crowd and immediately swing into the saddle.

"They're getting away!" Curt shouted.

I shoved one man aside and dodged another, then sprinted a few steps after them through the thinning crowd. But they had too great a start. We'd never catch them on foot. We had to fire, or they'd be gone. They dug their heels into the flanks of our horses, and the animals responded by lunging ahead.

"Take the one on the left!" I yelled. "Aim high so you don't hit anyone else."

Curt fired, then quickly fired again, and I saw Zimmer reel in the saddle and topple forward off his running horse.

Stoudt was leaning forward, making a smaller target as I drew back the hammer of my Colt, deliberately, and tried to level off on the bouncing figure. The hammer fell and my pistol roared.

For an instant I thought I'd hit him, because the horse reared. But the Morgan just danced and jumped around sideways. Stoudt was jerking the reins savagely and kicking him in the sides, trying to turn him. I sprang toward him again.

Then he spotted me and our eyes locked. He was less than fifteen yards away, his left side partly facing me. For an instant I could see the bitter hate of frustration in the cold eyes behind his glasses. It was like staring at a deadly snake, and for a second I was frozen into inaction and failed to see his right hand come up from the opposite side of his body, holding a gun. Just as my eye caught the glint of flames on the black gun barrel held across the saddle horn, he fired.

The movement of the horse must have ruined his aim, because white-hot pain seared my left cheek and earlobe, and I spun away to one side, rolling on the ground, trying to get into position to fire as I avoided any second or third shots.

But I needn't have bothered. The gun-shy Morgan went berserk. He bucked and kicked like a rodeo bronc. Stoudt clung desperately to the saddle horn as the horse tucked his head and spun in a tight circle, trying to rid himself of the terrifying thing on his back.

I watched from the ground as the horse threw his hindquarters into the air in one mighty buck and pitched Stoudt heels-over-head into the street.

But he was on his feet like a cat, and scrambled toward the livery stable as our horse galloped away up the street, dragging his reins.

"Where's Zimmer?" I yelled as Curt came running over to me.

"There he goes on foot. I winged him."

"Let's go."

Zimmer and Stoudt reached the door of the livery at almost the same time. But the padlock stopped them. They glanced back and saw us coming. All four of us fired hurried shots at nearly the same time. And all four of us missed. Our slugs thudded harmlessly into the wooden door behind them. They darted around the corner of the stable into the darkness, Zimmer holding his right arm.

We jumped for the darkness of the sheltered boardwalk on the same side of the street.

Breathing hard, I tried to count how many shots I had fired. I couldn't remember more than two.

"Reckon they ducked up that alley to make a break for the hills?"

"No. Since they're afoot, I'd bet they'll try to steal

some horses, or else are trying to lose themselves in town somewhere in all the confusion," Curt panted hoarsely as we hugged the wall.

"It's going to be tough flushing them out," I whispered back.

The firebell was clanging desperately somewhere in the distance. I heard the crash of falling timbers, and the flickering light grew even brighter. People were rushing into the street with lamps, chairs, trunks, and any valuables they could carry.

No one paid any attention to our shooting in the street. Gunfire and killing were common in Deadwood; fire was not.

"If only we could get Pierce or some of the men up here, we could cut 'em off."

"Everybody's down at the fire," Curt said. "Hope Cathy stays down there, even though they didn't find Stoudt." Curt looked over at me. "Hey, you're shot!" he said, alarmed, as he reached for the left side of my head. There was no pain, but his hand came away red. I felt the sticky mass that coated the side of my neck.

"The tip of your ear's shot away," Curt said, taking a closer look by the firelight. I gave him a big, clean bandanna from my pocket, and he quickly bound it around my head. "Press your hand against that ear. The bleeding should stop in a couple of minutes."

"Hell with that. What do we do now? Wait for them to come out?"

"No. They may be going down behind this row of buildings right now. We can't come this close and let 'em get away," Curt said.

"Looked like you got Zimmer in the arm or shoulder."

"Yeh. And I think one of them took a little buckshot when Cathy turned loose on 'em."

"Why don't I go down here to the next alley and cut around behind the buildings? Maybe we can box 'em in."

"Go ahead, but be careful," Curt cautioned.

"Right. If you hear any shooting, come a'running!"

I didn't have time to check my Colt as I took off running down the boardwalk toward the fire. At the first break in the solid row of wooden buildings I ducked into the shadows and slid quietly to the back of the building and looked around the corner. There was no one there. The trash piles and rain barrels stood silent and alone in the dimness. The only sounds were my own heavy breathing and the growing roar of the flames sweeping up the street, fed by the gusting wind and the resin-filled wooden buildings.

Were they still in the alley? Or had they climbed the hill? Or were they inside one of the buildings, possibly already past me?

The clinking of what sounded like a bottle jerked my head around. I had been looking up the street toward the alley where Zimmer and Stoudt had disappeared, but the sound came from the other direction, about three buildings down. I strained my eyes. Was it a dog, or a rat, that had knocked something in a trash pile? But then I caught a glimpse of a dark figure disappearing into a building, and heard a door bang shut.

I fired three quick shots into the air to call Curt, and then began to reload. Before I could even finish and snap shut the loading gate, he was at my side.

"I think they just went in the back door of the bakery," I said.

"Let's go."

Making no attempt to be quiet, we ran for the windowless back door of the bakery and stopped. Sweat was streaming down my face, stinging the bullet burn on my cheek. My shirt was soaked.

"Don't go busting in there. Could be an ambush."

"We've got them cornered against that fire, unless they get across the street."

The fire, like a searing red and yellow dragon, came roaring up the gulch, devouring everything in its path and growing larger and stronger every minute. It had already reached the hardware store next door to where we stood. The searing heat was so intense I had to turn away and press myself against the bakery wall.

"Let's give it a few seconds and then burst in. They

may think they've shaken us. In any case, they can't stay in there long, or they'll burn up."

"Hell, they may have gone right on out the front door."

"Let's go, then," Curt said. "And go in shooting to cover us."

I put my hand on the door latch, eased it up, and then flung it back, and our guns roared together as we leaped inside. I heard some scrambling near the front of the room where the fire was throwing a bright glow through the front windows.

Two shots in quick succession answered us, and I felt a slug tear through the top of my boot and burn the skin of my leg as I dropped to the floor.

"Give it up, Stoudt!" Curt yelled. Three shots was the only reply.

Smoke was pouring in the back door, which still stood open, and through the cracks in the wall. The roar of the conflagration rose to a crescendo as it created its own huge draft and consumed the adjacent hardware store.

What followed next is somewhat blurred in my memory. We had taken cover crouched down behind boxes of fresh bread stacked on heavy wooden tables. This probably saved our lives. All I could recall later was the stunning concussion of an explosion hitting me like a solid blow on my left side. The next instant I was on the floor against the opposite wall with splintered boards and pieces of iron stove falling all around me. Then, everything went black.

I must have been unconscious only a few seconds. I awoke to a feeling of suffocation. Half the room was afire. Shredded loaves of bread, charred and splintered wood, and an iron stove door partially covered me. The heat and smoke were unbelievable. Blood was running down my face from a fresh gash in my scalp but I scarcely felt it.

My first impulse was to escape—to get outside to air— but then I thought of Curt. I wiped the blood from my eyes with a sleeve and shook my throbbing head to clear my senses. There was a ringing in my ears. The deadly danger sharpened my wits instantly, and it took only a second or two to find Curt a few feet from me. He was conscious, but stunned and uncomprehending. The room was bright as day. I had to hug the floor to suck what oxygen was still available.

Curt tried to sit up, but I dragged him down next to me and yelled, "Curt! Are you okay?" He stared at me blankly. I ran my hands over him quickly when he didn't reply. When I touched his left arm, he winced and cried out in pain. His sleeve was shredded and his forearm was bent at an odd angle. The sharp pain seemed to bring him to his senses.

"Let me pull you. We have to get out!" I shouted at him. He nodded, biting his lips against the pain.

Crawling backward, I kicked debris out of our way and pulled him by his good arm as he lay on his right side. His cries of anguish every time we bumped something hardly registered in my mind.

Parts of both the front and back walls were blown out, and the sagging ceiling was a mass of flames. I thought only of what would happen if it collapsed on us before we reached the front. Blood and perspiration were blinding me, and the thickening smoke was beginning to make my head reel again. I tried to hold my breath, but the exertion of crawling and dragging Curt was too much—I had to breathe. Every intake of breath was searing hot, and I began to panic. Letting go of Curt, I turned around and threw boards and pots and utensils out of my way and lunged for the street. A quick gust of wind fanned the flames and smoke back from me for a few seconds, and I gulped sweet, fresh, life-giving air. A half-dozen deep breaths, a sleeve across my streaming face, and I fought down my instinctive fear and dove back on hands and knees for Curt. He had passed out, which made it a little easier to drag him to safety.

I finally tugged him to the middle of the street, and the strength seemed to suddenly drain out of me. I flopped over on my back, arms outspread, and stared into the black night sky between the rows of burning buildings. Flames appeared to be shooting as high as the hills on either side of the gulch.

With a roar even louder than the fire, the remaining roof of the bakery collapsed, throwing a beautiful shower

of sparks high overhead. I watched this display of fire-
works with a detached air, as if viewing it from a safe
distance.

Suddenly, I was aware of men and voices around me.

"God, what a blast!"

"Yeah, Henson had black powder stored in the hardware in spite of all the warnings," someone answered.
"Just blew flamin' stuff all over town. Damn! There goes
the rest o' the buildings we mighta saved."

"Ain't no way we coulda saved anything without blastin'
a firebreak somewhere. The fire wagon burned first off."

"Yeh. With this wind, nothing can help. Get some o' the
boys up to the livery and turn them horses out."

I could hear voices all around, but couldn't seem to
move or speak. I imagined myself in the bottom of a pit
with the walls of hell surrounding me. The whole wild
display seemed staged for my benefit.

The voices were coming closer.

"Hey, Charlie, this one's dead. Musta got blowed plumb
outta one o' them buildings."

I rolled over on my stomach and pushed myself up on
both elbows. I felt very light-headed. The men I had heard
talking were bent over a form a few yards away. I began
crawling toward them. Three men saw me and ceased examining the corpse and quickly came to me.

"This one's still alive. Boy, what a mess! Hold on,
mister. You'll be all right."

"Curt. My friend. Here. Over here," I said weakly,
motioning toward his still form.

"Take it easy. We'll get him," one of them said.

Friendly hands were swabbing my face with a wet cloth.
I pushed the hand away, fighting my dizziness.

"That man who's dead over there."

I struggled to my feet and reeled toward the figure in
the street. Yes. It was seared, blackened, and bloody, but
I had seen that face too many times to be mistaken—it was
Major George Zimmer!

Then I felt myself falling and arms catching me.

CHAPTER 20

"The two of you look a little strange with most of your hair and your eyebrows singed off," Cathy remarked to Curt and me two days later.

"Better my hair than my head," Curt laughed.

"If that explosion didn't damage our hearing, we should be as good as new in a few weeks," I said.

We were sitting with a large group of townspeople on makeshift log benches in front of a row of tents on a grassy area near the edge of town. Or rather, what had been the town. Heaps of rubble, ashes, and blackened, smoking timbers were all that remained of Deadwood.

"I still can't believe it," Wiley said, shaking his head. "It was gone so fast. Only about thirty buildings on the slopes were spared. It got Mrs. Hayes's place."

"I guess no more than three people were killed by it," Pat Burnett added. His massive form moved about, in and out of a nearby tent as he poured free dipperfuls of whiskey along a plank bar for anyone who wanted it. Several women were also dispensing coffee and water to a lot of sweating men who were taking a lunch break from the business of cleaning up. Wiley held out his tin cup for a refill. "At least someone had the good sense to save a couple barrels of the 'water of life,'" he said, smacking his lips at the taste.

"About a ton of flour was saved, too," Cathy added. "And there are men out hunting for meat right now."

"Well, it's an ill wind that doesn't blow somebody some good," Curt quoted, shifting his splinted left arm in its sling so he could reach the sandwich Cathy handed him. "I don't think anybody's going to hold it against us for starting that fire, considering that their stages and their gold will be safe now."

The men from nearby towns and camps had brought their wagons and tools to help clear the smoking ruins and to start the rebuilding. No sawmills had been touched by the fire, since they stood too far from town. And they were going full blast. The tortured whine of saws ripping new lumber rose and fell over all other noises.

Most of the buildings in the new Deadwood would be made of something more durable, the mayor had assured the stunned townspeople—stone, and bricks made from the irritating gumbo. He also promised that an adequate water supply would be available to fight any future fires.

"Where's Stoudt?" I asked nobody in particular.

"Sheriff Pierce and a few deputies took him and Stumpy McCoy and about six of his gang and started for Cheyenne in one of the Wells Fargo coaches about an hour ago," Mortimer replied. "When I saw Stoudt coming down the street the other night, I almost didn't recognize him," Mortimer added. "He was staggering like a drunk and he was totally black with soot. His glasses were gone and his clothes were in rags. Somebody ran over to help him, and then I realized who he was. As soon as he'd been treated for minor burns and shock, I arrested him. By yesterday he was lucid, and I started pressuring him to tell me where Stumpy's gang was holed up."

"Did they get the fake shipment?" Wiley asked.

"No. Jason Thomas got to Stumpy in time to warn them off." He grinned. "I guess that wagon load of rocks will get through safely to Cheyenne."

"Some of Sheriff Pierce's posse went through the ashes of Stoudt's bank after they cooled down yesterday, and found the safe intact. He wouldn't give us the combination until Pierce ordered it blasted open. They didn't find anything out of order there—just three hundred or so buckskin pokes of dust tagged with individuals' names, waiting to be melted and shipped. But a search of his house turned up a tin box with some scorched ledgers detailing a record of payments to S. McCoy, G. Zimmer, and an R. Telford. It also showed a tremendous amount of gold received by himself. He still refused to say anything except that it was his own returns from private investment.

"We told him Zimmer had been killed in the explosion, and that if he wanted to face murder and robbery charges alone and see Stumpy get away with the rest of the gold, he could. At first he pretended not to know who Cassius 'Stumpy' McCoy was. But then the idea of taking the punishment all alone finally got to him. He confessed and told us where Stumpy was. He led the posse right to a cavern less than a dozen miles from here, and the gang, not expecting anyone, had not posted a guard. They were all captured, along with about a half-million dollars worth of gold, most of which had been smelted and recast right there. Some of the ingots still had the Wells Fargo stamping on them. Plenty of evidence to convict. That's where we found your watches and a lot of other personal things that had been taken from stage passengers.

"Nobody had known of this natural cavern; that's how the robbers could disappear so quickly without a trace. It was plenty big enough for horses and a good stock of provisions. Probably could've housed half the town in there."

"Stoudt looked like a wealthy man. Why did he get involved with a bunch of robbers?" I asked.

"He wasn't so well off as he appeared. He was heavily in debt. For a generous cut of the profits, he got the help of McCoy's gang to rob the gold shipments. Then Stoudt and his partners were using their share of the loot to buy up promising mines in the Hills. He was also paying off his own debts. As soon as he was in a good solid financial position, he was going to pay off the gang and send them on their way. If they wouldn't leave voluntarily, he himself was going to leave and assume a new identity in some eastern city. From there he could manage his developing mines through a dummy company."

"How did he know all about these treasure shipments in advance?" Curt wanted to know.

"We had a little trouble getting that out of him, but we found a couple of telegrams in the cavern that had been sent to Stoudt from Cheyenne. They were apparently routine bank business, but they were really coded messages about the dates, routes, times, amounts, hiding places, and number of guards for two different gold shipments at different times. Written above each line of the coded telegrams, in Stoudt's own hand, was the translation —very damning evidence that Stumpy failed to destroy." He laughed, rubbing the silver stubble on his cheeks. "I told you Stumpy was slippery, but not too intelligent."

"You never said who his contact was."

"Oh, yes. The other name in the ledger—Telford— turned out to be the Wells Fargo agent, Bundy's counterpart, in Cheyenne. Bundy never suspected and routinely notified Telford in advance of every shipment. The agent turned right around and sent a coded wire to Stoudt, who tipped off Jason Thomas, who carried the information to McCoy."

"Simple enough. But how did Zimmer fit into all this?"

"When General Buck's troops came through here last September, Zimmer met Stoudt. Turns out he and Stoudt had known each other as kids years ago. Grew up in the same German community in Wisconsin. They hit it off right away. When Zimmer got suspended from duty, pending a court-martial, he faced the end of his career, the loss of his pension, and a dishonorable discharge. He was thinking of recouping his fortunes by looking up his old friend Stoudt. Stoudt took him into his scheme as a partner, along with Telford at Cheyenne."

"Right. After all, what are friends for?" Wiley asked dryly.

"Did Stoudt have anything to do with shooting you?"

"Don't know for sure, but he may break down and tell us yet, since he's already facing charges of murder, attempted murder, and robbery. I have a hunch he put Jason Thomas up to it. Even though my mission was kept pretty quiet, even within the company, I imagine Telford was the one who identified me."

"By the way," Curt said, glancing around at the crowd with a concerned look, "has everyone been accounted for? I haven't seen K.J. since the fire."

"He's okay," Wiley replied. "I saw him yesterday afternoon and again this morning. He was really busy helping the men clean up. In fact, I saw him with Missus Hayes and one of the miners who hung around her place a lot and helped her. They had a couple of wheelbarrows made out of pieces of sluice boxes, and were hauling off loads of ashes."

"Good. I'm glad to know the kid and Missus Hayes weren't hurt."

I glanced around at the swarms of men shoveling, digging, salvaging a few useful items from the heaps of black and gray ashes. Teams of mules were dragging heavy timbers and pulling down the remainders of brick chimneys.

"You know," I remarked, "I'll bet a man could leave here today and come back in six months and never know this for the same place."

"You're right. And it's a bit sad in a way," Mortimer said. "I think this fire will probably knock some of the raw edge off Deadwood. With the Hills officially given up by the Indians last month, this town'll be a different place by the time it's all rebuilt. A little tamer and more settled, maybe. A little less placer mining, and more hard-rock mining—and more stamp mills as the surface gold starts to play out. The Homestake is already developing that way. And the Father DeSmet, the Golden Star, the Giant, and Old Abe will be into the deep shafts and tunneling before long, and then most of the mining will be done by men working for wages—Cornishmen and the like. Developing a mine takes lots of capital and know-how. But it's not as exciting as those first discoveries, when it's every man for himself and everyone, potentially, has an equal chance."

"Stoudt saw it coming and wanted to raise some quick, easy, illegal money to buy into these mines," Curt said.

"Speaking of that," Wiley said, "what are we going to do with our claim? Just keep sluicing until we come up empty, and then start digging? Most of our gold probably washed down from somewhere higher up. There may not be any veins under our section of creek."

"I've been giving that some thought," Curt replied, adding some water to his tin cup of whiskey and sipping it. "I want to discuss this with the three of you. What do you think of the idea of possibly selling about twenty percent of our two adjoining claims to some miners to finish it up or develop whatever it leads to?

"Personally, I've got some plans of my own." He reached for Cathy's hand with his good right hand. "I've asked Cathy to marry me, and she's accepted."

Cathy held out her left hand for us to see the delicate gold ring. I took a closer look at the finely crafted design. The slender gold band curved gracefully at the top into two grape leaves fanning out from a tiny bunch of grapes. The tiny leaves were a pale red and green in color.

"A young jeweler down at Rosenthal's came up with that design," Curt explained. "The colors are obtained by alloying the gold with copper and silver. He's produced quite a few of them over the past few months. That design of his in Black Hills gold is already becoming popular."

"Beautiful," I commented, rubbing my fingers over the roughened surface of the leaves.

"I can't let a girl get away who's as good with a shotgun as she is," Curt continued. "I may hire her out to Wells Fargo."

"And I'm a terrific cook, too," Cathy retorted.

"By the way, where did you get that double-barreled gun?"

"When you didn't come down right away, and we heard voices in the hallway, Wiley and I decided we'd better get up there quick. Wiley had a revolver, but I wasn't armed, so I just ran behind the desk and grabbed the shotgun I'd seen the night clerk stand in the corner when he came on duty. He hollered at me, but I just kept on going. Checked to make sure both barrels were loaded on our way up the stairs."

"I'm sure glad you did. If it weren't for the two of you, we wouldn't be sitting here right now," I said.

"Anyway, I'd like to settle right here in Deadwood for a time," Curt went on. "With my engineering degree, I can foresee plenty of work—building, bridge, and mine-tunnel construction. I may even look into the possibility of working for the railroad. They'll probably be running a line in here within a few years if this area grows the way I think it will."

"Congratulations," Wiley said, grinning broadly. "I can't think of a better match. But for the life of me, I can't figure out which one of you is going to be the boss."

Cathy made a face at him and put her arm around the seated Curt's shoulders.

"What about your troubles with the army?" I asked.

"I think that would hurt me back East," Curt replied, his lean face serious. "But out here, they look more at a man's skills and current behavior, rather than at his past. I know of several sheriffs and marshals who used to be on the wrong side of the law.

"But I still think I was right in my actions. In any case, I'm not going to hide. If the Army wants to come looking for me, I'll be here. And I'll even face a court-martial if they want me to. In effect, I've already resigned my commission. Zimmer's dead, so his testimony won't be there to hurt me. If they want to give me a dishonorable discharge for the record, there's probably nothing I can do about it, but I want to get my side of the story on the official transcript of the trial for anyone who might be interested in it in the future—like our kids."

"Talking about kids, look who's coming," I said, pointing at K.J., who had set his empty wheelbarrow down to come get a drink of water from a nearby barrel.

"Hey, you're really working," Cathy said to him. "The way you're going at it, somebody must be paying you to clean up this whole town by yourself."

K.J. put the dipper back in the barrel and wiped the back of his hand across his mouth, smearing soot on his cheek. The black eyes gleamed in the round face as he came over to our group.

"Nobody's paying me," he said. "We're paying ourselves. Since all of you are good friends of mine, I'll let you in on our secret. But please don't tell anyone else until we're through."

We all promised.

He lowered his voice. "That miner who's helping me and Missus Hayes gave us the idea. We're picking out certain stores and saloons and washing out the ashes of those places in his sluice box. And we're finding gold dust," he whispered. "That miner says Missus Hayes was good to him when he was down on his luck, and he wanted to help her build her house back and get her a good stake. He says before we're through, we should get about two thousand pennyweight of gold out of there!"

"Two-thousand pennyweight!" Curt exclaimed, doing some quick mental calculations. "That's upward of four thousand dollars or more."

"Now, that's what I call enterprising," Wiley said.

"By the way, part of that thousand dollar reward for capturing those stage robbers will go to you for helping us," Curt said. "We couldn't have done it without you."

The boy's round face split into a huge grin, showing his dimples. "Thank you!" he said. "I gotta go now. Missus Hayes is waiting on me." He waved and went to trundle off the wheelbarrow, which was almost bigger than he was.

"I'd like to adopt that kid and get an early start on a family," Curt said, half to himself. And then aloud he asked, "What are your plans, Matt and Wiley? Going to stay on here?"

"As for me," I answered, "I'll stay for the wedding if it isn't too far off. But these winters are a little rough for me. I've been hearing about some promising silver strikes down in the Arizona Territory. I've never been in that part of the country, and I'd like to check 'em out. I want to get a good look at different parts of the West and see what's available before I settle down. You know, I never did get a reply from my old newspaper. Guess they're not going to pay me for my summer's work."

"If you don't mind the company, I'd like to tag along with you," Wiley said. "I haven't got any definite plans. Besides, you may need some looking after. I was over that part of the country a few years back before the Apaches got rough, and I had to get out. Besides, I've

got enough from my share of dad's inheritance to give us
a good stake and plenty of time to look around."

It was a comforting thought to know I would have an
experienced guide, and I stuck out my hand.

"Done," I said. "You be my scout and guide, and I'll
try to keep you out of trouble."

He grinned that boyish grin and gripped my hand.

"Looks like we've each got a full-time job."